Pried

by

J L Wilson

A Remembered Classics Romance

Pried

Cover Art by *Kim Mendoza*

The Wild Rose Press, Inc.
PO Box 708
Adams Basin, NY 14410-0708
Visit us at www.thewildrosepress.com

Publishing History
First Crimson Rose Edition, 2019
Print ISBN 978-1-5092-2536-1
Digital ISBN 978-1-5092-2537-8

A Remembered Classics Romance
Published in the United States of America

Ann drew in a deep breath, getting ready to blast me with her wrath. She stepped closer to me, but her shoe caught on the area rug and she twisted slightly. When she faced me again, she merely sighed instead of raging. "It's so sad that you won't admit the truth. You're so pitiable, Jane. You should learn from your mistakes, not try to sweep them under a rug." She set her plastic wine glass on my side table and turned to the French doors. "Oh, Fitz. There you are." She smiled at Dr. Williams and went to join him in the doorway. "Jane and I were just chatting."

"So I heard. Your mother was asking where you went. I think she'd like a ride home." Williams turned to me. "Thank you for your hospitality. I enjoyed myself."

"We can drop her off on the way to my house." Ann swept from the room, acting as regal as a queen. She stood on the porch, glaring at me.

I crossed my arms and glared right back at her. "She always gets the last word," I muttered. "Just once I'd like to beat her in an argument."

Williams took a step toward me. "I admire a woman who stands up for herself," he said in a low, confidential voice. "I've never been fond of victims. Well done, Miss Austin. Well done." He left, leaning close to Ann to hear her complaints. Just before they walked out of sight, he glanced back at me and winked.

Dedication

To all you Master Gardeners out there
bringing beauty to the world
one garden at a time

Other Titles by J L Wilson

Autographs, Abductions, and A-list Authors
Brownies, Bodies, and Breaking the Code
Candy, Corpses, and Classified Ads
Daisies, Deadly Force, and Disastrous Divorce
Disputes
Ex-Wives, Extortion and Erotic First Editions
Foxgloves, Fancy Fungus, and Fatal Family Feuds
Homicide, Hostages, and Hot Rod Restoration
Human Touch
Leap of Faith
Lilacs, Litigation, and Lethal Love Affairs
Living Proof
Mayhem, Marriage, and Murderous Mystery
Manuscripts
Murder and Mayhem (Boxed Set)
PhDs, Pornography and Premeditated Murder
Resorts, Regrets, and Returning to Love
Sun, Surf and Sandy Strangulation
~*~

Other "Remembered Classics" Titles:
Woulds
Flyer
Dogged
Laked
~*~

All are published by The Wild Rose Press, Inc.
www.thewildrosepress.com

Chapter 1

"Listen to this," I said, reading from the local newspaper. "*Ms. Jane Austin inherited a stellar literary name, yet it is a pity that she didn't inherit a stellar literary talent. Her first book,* The Gentleman and the Lady, *is sadly lacking in anything that constitutes a fine literary work.*" I lowered the newspaper and regarded my good friend, Ben Jaines. "Of course, it isn't a fine literary work. He missed the point. It's a romance novel. Duh. Different genre, dufus."

Ben glared at the newspaper. "Did I tell you that my brother-in-law knows him?"

"Really?" I took a sip of wine. "He knows Dr. D.F. Williams, of Derby College? The new reviewer for our hometown rag?"

"Yeah, they went to school together out East. George mentioned it when he asked me for money again." Ben regarded me with sad-eyed concern. "I don't know what to do."

I closed the *Barn and Bugle,* our local newspaper. Ben was often hit up for money by his feckless brother-in-law, George Wick. Ben inherited all the common sense in his family and almost all the money. His other siblings were relatively well off, but his youngest sister Lydia went through cash like water running through her fingers. She was in her forties now but still acted like the reckless teenager she used to be.

1

"You shouldn't bail them out again." Ben and I had been friends for decades, but his lack of spine where his family was concerned still irritated me.

"I know." He sipped his bourbon and set down his glass. "But it's hard to turn your back on your sister."

"Lydia knows it, too." I suppose I shouldn't criticize. I had no siblings or family to speak of. My parents were dead, and my ex-husband lived far from Longbarn, Iowa, where I currently resided. I changed the subject. "Speaking of Derby College, how are things at my alma mater?"

Ben peered at my garden, just a few feet from my screened porch at the back of my house, where we sat on a beautiful June evening. He pushed his curly light brown hair back from his forehead, but it had a mind of its own despite his best efforts to tame it. Ben always seemed a bit surprised, his brown eyes wide and somehow innocent looking. He was one of the nicest people I've ever met, and I swear he didn't have a mean bone in his body.

"Things are fine at school," he said, staring intently at my flower bed. "Summer school starts on Monday."

"And how is Miss Charlotte Bing?"

His cheeks darkened with color. Ben was my age—fifty-five—but there were times he acted like a schoolboy. "She's teaching school this summer."

"And so are you. How convenient." I couldn't help teasing him. Ben taught American history at the nearby private college, and Dr. Charlotte Bing, a relative newcomer, taught British history. Ben pined for her from afar for an entire school year. The man had a case of terminal shyness where women were concerned. "You are bringing her to my party on Saturday, right?"

"Well, we're riding together at least."

He seemed so glum I wanted to laugh aloud, but I managed to restrain myself. "As long as you're together, that's what matters, right?"

"I suppose." Ben swirled the bourbon around in his glass. "We should go soon. The Sierra Club guy wanted us to get there early to hear the other speakers. Have you seen Mr. Collins? He's supposed to talk tonight, too, but nobody's heard from him."

"I haven't seen him."

"Did you call him?"

"You know, just because he lives in my neighborhood, that doesn't mean he and I are friends." I took a sip of wine, avoiding Ben's gaze. "No, I didn't call him." Old Man Collins lived a half mile south from me and was a thoroughly unpleasant man given to snide comments about our neighbor, Catherine Burge, a wealthy widow who acted like she owned the entire subdivision. Not surprising, really, since she used to own the land on which most of the subdivision sat.

"Maybe you should stop by his house. He's old. Maybe something happened."

"Old? He's only seventy or so." My encroaching fifty-fifth birthday was beginning to alter my perspective on what constituted "elderly."

I got up and went to the edge of the porch, peering at the wetlands in the distance. My house was on a slight hill, and I had a bit of a view through the trees at the farm lands and houses abutting the marsh. I couldn't see Collins' house from here, though, because Mrs. Burge's house blocked my view.

"You know what I mean," Ben said. "Maybe he fell into the water or something. He loves to prowl around the fen. We really need all the supporters we can get tonight."

That was a real possibility. Collins' house wasn't far from a large fen, a prairie wetland area adjacent to a small wildlife refuge. During the winter and in the sweltering summer months, a wooden walkway was high above the vegetation. The walkway sometimes disappeared during rainy times. Although it was now June and the weather was heating up, we had had several weeks of off-and-on rain. It was quite possible Collins went for a walk, strayed from the path, and even now might be mired in a bog.

"I'll knock on his door," I said grudgingly. "But I won't go looking for him. Mosquitos are starting to hatch."

Ben stood. "I'll get to the meeting early, so I can listen to the opposition and take notes."

I picked up my empty wine glass and Ben's glass then walked back into the house with him. "Make sure to get here by seven for the party. It should be fun; I've invited just about everybody I know."

"Did you invite Ann Burge?"

I shot Ben a suspicious glance, but he was all innocence. "Yes, I did. She lives in the neighborhood and she teaches creative writing at the college so I figured, why not? Have her come to my launch party for my first published novel and let her critique me if she wants."

"You and she have been competing for students for years. I'm surprised you invited her."

"Competing for students?" I put a hand on my bosom in mock dismay. "I teach creative writing at the Community College. She teaches at the Real College.

How could I compete with that?"

"You compete very well," he said with a grin. "Seems to me your classes are always full."

"As are hers," I pointed out while I tucked our glasses into the dishwasher. "Be careful. The cat's behind you."

He stepped to one side, almost treading on Persuasion, my part-Persian, part-mystery-parentage cat. After a minor confusion of paws and feet, we headed for the front door. "Ann and I have a very cordial relationship," I said. "We cordially detest each other."

"You'd better watch it. She might slip you a mickey. She has to be jealous of the fact you have a three-book deal and your first book just released."

I shrugged. "They're romance novels. As far as she's concerned, it's not real fiction."

"Is she bringing a date?"

I pulled open the front door, letting in a heady mix of lavender and wood mulch from my front herb garden with a piquant hint of sage thrown in. "She did say she might bring a guest. Why?"

Ben's deep brown eyes—puppy eyes—sparkled with mischief. "She's dating Dr. Williams. The book reviewer."

"Seriously?" I grinned. "Well, that might be interesting. Is he new? I don't recognize the name." I knew most of the English faculty at Derby College. I was a student there, lo, those many years ago. I left for the wider world then returned to teach there until the scandal ten years earlier.

"He filled in after Dr. Knight died. He teaches criticism and 19th century English novels. He used to live near Boston. I think he taught at a private college there."

"Lit crit and Early Brits," I murmured. "A heady combination. What's he doing in Iowa?"

Ben dug his hands into his jeans pockets and hunched his shoulders, a pose I recognized. "He and Charlotte are friends. She recommended him for the position here. From what I've heard, he's well-off, so teaching is sort of a sideline for him, not a career."

"Oh." Poor Ben. He was so forlorn. I put an arm around his waist and gave him a hug. "He's dating Ann, so there's nothing to worry about."

Ben hugged me back. "I know. See you at City Hall. Don't be late." He hurried down the front walk to his car.

I closed the door. Persuasion peeked at me from my study, where he had taken refuge. It was located off the foyer with a door leading to the side porch and my rocking chair there. He loved sitting by the door to view the Great Outside. "Come on, P-cat. Time for treats."

He recognized the word *treat* and led the way back to the kitchen where I gave him a couple of seafood chewies. He settled himself in the dining nook to gaze at birds clustered around my bird feeders.

I crossed the living room and went into my bedroom to prepare for the evening's meeting. I changed my jeans and golf shirt for a lightweight denim skirt and a blue summer sweater shot through with pale red-gold lines, the same color as my hair. Low-heeled blue sandals completed my ensemble.

I went to the attached bathroom to assess myself in the mirror. My hair was still mostly red-gold, but I had more than a few silver strands mixed in. My skin was relatively unlined and pale, thanks to my slavish devotion to sunscreen, but there were telltale grooves around my mouth and my dark amber eyes. And I was still slender, a must for someone only five feet three, but gravity was starting to pull a few of my parts downward, especially my rather generous breasts.

I dabbed on eye makeup, wondering where this self-critique came from. I seldom indulged in that kind of evaluation. Then I remembered my visitor and my mood lightened. Ben's romantic woes probably put notions in my head.

I brushed on some blusher, then left the master bedroom after checking that the french doors leading to the porch were locked. I went back to the living room and found the newspaper where I dropped it on the coffee table. I turned to the last inside page.

Her casual writing style is certainly easy to read, and her characters are well developed, but her plot lacks finesse and subtlety. The tired trope of mistaken identity and misunderstanding between the classes is unsuitable for a more modern-day novel, and because of that, the reader is left to wonder why the hero and heroine are even attracted to one another, unless, of course, it's for the sex, which is lovingly and elaborately described in the pages of this novel.

"Your writing style leaves a bit to be desired. Talk about your run-on sentences. Don't you know how to write a book review, Dr. D. F. Williams?" I dropped the paper and went to my den. I found my *Directory of Staff and Faculty* for Derby College, located in Manortown, about twenty miles to the east.

Dr. D. Fitzgerald Williams was in the listings for the Department of English. "Ben was right," I said to

Persuasion, positioned at the door staring at the birds. "He teaches rhetoric. And Regency literature."

Oh, well. It was a pity my first book review in my hometown paper came from a pompous know-it-all, but I wouldn't let it bother me.

Much.

I scribbled his name on my invitation list for my book launch party next to Ann Burge's name. It might be interesting to argue narrative theory with the asshole. Cheered by the thought, I left the house and backed my blue Mini Cooper out of my garage, pausing at my mailbox across the street to pick up that afternoon's missives. A bulky manila envelope, undoubtedly full of a dense retirement investment summary, was jammed into the box along with a few letters. I tucked everything into my leather book bag and drove along Rosings Drive, the main street winding through our subdivision of Mansfield Park.

Two other roads, Rosings Way and Rosings Lane, bisected the big circle that was our neighborhood. Mrs. Burge and her husband had owned the land on which our houses now sat and divided it into two-acre tracts. Most of the houses were like mine, smaller Craftsman-style homes on heavily wooded lots, but there were a few McMansions scattered amongst their lesser sisters.

I drove south past the Burge mansion on my right and made the right turn at the end of the street to loop past Mr. Collins' house on my left. His home was a single-story ranch-style house sitting far back from the road, his "drive" a rutted and winding gravel lane thirty or forty yards long. The Burges owned the land north of Rosings Drive, and Collins owned the land south of it, mostly consisting of the marshy area and a few acres of farm land where a horse and donkey still grazed. Collins' stable and house were on a slight hill, but even so, I know he had water in his basement from time to time.

I drove carefully along the twisting lane to his home and parked in front of his garage. When I approached the house, I stayed on the stone walkway, careful not to step off into the muddy soil next to it. No answer when I rang the doorbell and no way to see into the house given the heavy wooden door. I went to the garage, but the windows in it were too high for me to see through.

I walked around the right side of the house where the stone path led to the back yard, a sloping patch of lawn. In the distance, about fifty yards away, was the fen, a low, green expanse of land stretching a half mile to the verdant Wildlife Area and Botanical Preserve. The Lea River was in the distance, west of the preserve. It flowed north-south here, then made a sharp turn about a mile south and flowed east-west on the southern part of Longbarn.

"Mr. Collins!" I called. The only answer was silence then an occasional rumble from the toads in the marsh. Most of the fen appeared to be covered with greenery, but when I walked down Collins' hillside, I saw the rough wooden walkways were still above the water moving sluggishly underneath. Not far above the water, but still visible, at least.

"Mr. Collins!" I yelled again, cupping my hands to send my words across the fen. The sharp tang of rotting vegetation and stagnant water wafted to me, borne on a gentle southern breeze. The odor was usually contained here at ground level, but occasionally I could even catch a whiff of it at my house on top of the hill.

I turned to peer back up the slope to Collins' house. There was no sign of the crotchety old man who lived alone. His wife died years ago, and their only child, Luke, had moved away. I walked up the hill to the patio at the back of his house. "Mr. Collins! Are you home?"

A pair of binoculars sat on a table next to a lawn chair under the patio awning. I used them to gaze at the fen, moving the glasses slowly from side to side. At one point on my left, near the top of the hill that formed the pasture, I thought I saw a bit of bright red. I focused on it and realized it was a tree with a strip of ribbon or tape on it.

Perhaps construction tape on a tree? I wasn't sure. I focused again. The tree was an enormous old oak, situated at the edge of the pasture and abutting the marsh. It was hard to see unless I moved because it was nearly obscured by the other trees in front of it.

I glanced at my watch. It was almost seven o'clock and the meeting was starting. I put down the glasses and walked back to my car, stopping again to ring the doorbell. When I got no reply, I returned to my car and drove away from the subdivision, making a right turn on Rosings Lane which led me to the county road and from there into town.

Longbarn's City Hall, a one-story modern brick building, was situated near the center of our small town on the corner of 8th Avenue and 8th Street. I parked in the lot behind City Hall. The city park was across the street, and I dashed over to take a moment and admire the flower beds. I was a master gardener and assisted in the layout and installation of the design. Four beds bordered the circular center of the park, with rainbow colors starting in one bed and continuing through the others. The effect was subtle but lovely, especially when viewed from the elevated gazebo in the center of the block.

Several other citizens were in the park, enjoying the balmy June evening, and I spent a pleasant few minutes chatting with other gardeners about the installation. Consequently, I was later than I planned to be when I walked into the large room at City Hall. The city council normally used the space when it met, but several folding "walls" were moved so now it was essentially a large rectangular auditorium. Rows of hard blue plastic chairs were aligned on the left, center, and right, facing the front with aisles between the sections.

A tall man was at the microphone speaking when I slipped into the room. The large skylights let in soft evening light, making the wood tones of the podium and the desk where the mayor sat glow with warmth. The number of people there surprised me. The room was almost full, which meant a hundred or more people showed up for this informational meeting. The proposed road construction project generated a lot of animosity in the town and the turnout proved that.

I made my way around the perimeter to other committee members seated near the microphone, which was placed on the left in a front corner so the speaker could face the entire room. I didn't recognize the man speaking, and I think I would have remembered him. He had curly dark gray hair brushed back from his forehead and large dark eyes behind horn-rimmed glasses. His good looks were noticeable, but it was his voice that caught my attention. He spoke in a low, confident tone with no hesitation or self-consciousness.

"...at the expense of a handful of turtles," he said. "I'm sure it must seem callous to some of the environmentalists here, but don't we need to consider what is best for the most people? This road will have a very positive impact on the west side of town. It will open up acres of land for development and shopping and..."

I tuned him out. I'd heard this bullshit argument more times than I could count. I took a seat next to Ben, who listened intently to the man, jotting notes on a pad balanced on his knee.

"Where have you been?" he whispered without taking his eyes from his notepad.

"I was detained." I peeked at Ben's notepad. *Professor from school; they benefit; biased. Can't be trusted to have an objective opinion.*

"He's with the college?" I whispered.

Ben tapped the notepad. *Professor.* Then he scribbled, *Williams.*

I sat up straighter in surprise. What was my nasty book reviewer doing speaking at a town meeting?

"...have a vested interest in this project. Not only does the college own some of the land near the proposed route, but I also own land there. Yes, my land values will rise substantially if this area is developed. I admit that readily." Williams shrugged broad shoulders, his gray-and-black sports coat rising with the motion. He was nattily dressed in black slacks, the sports coat and a dark gray shirt with gray-and-black striped tie. It was like a Calvin Klein ad in *Where To Retire* magazine. The guy was the picture of wealthy senior man-about-town. It was a pity his pedantic prose didn't match his appearance.

"While profit is a motivator for me, I am also interested in what's best for the future of this community. I'm a newcomer here, but perhaps it's because I'm new that I'm able to view this project with a more objective eye than some of the people who live near the area." He glanced at Ben and our group when he said that, a faint smile making deep dimples appear at the sides of his mouth.

"Asshole," Ben muttered. He also wore a sports coat, but it wasn't as well-fitted as the one Williams wore. They were probably about the same age, mid-fifties, and they both wore eyeglasses, but that's where the resemblance ended. Ben was plain and a blend-in-the-crowd kind of guy. Williams was handsome and polished.

I immediately felt guilty at making such a comparison. Ben had a heart of gold and was a tireless volunteer. "Don't worry. We have the Sierra Club behind us."

Ben nodded, but he didn't appear cheered by the thought.

"Thank you for allowing me a chance to speak," Williams said, stepping back from the podium where the microphone sat. "I appreciate the opportunity to air my views on such an important matter for our community."

"Our community," Ben muttered. "Asshole lives in Manortown, near the campus."

"Thank you, Professor, for expressing your opinion." Our mayor, a middle-aged man with a propensity to drink, peered at a paper in front of him on the table where he and the other council members sat. "We have one more speaker to talk in favor of our proposal then we'll have a short break and hear from those opposed. I believe the county engineer is speaking next, is that right?"

I turned in my seat to check the back of the room. Williams was almost to the exit. When he neared it, a woman stood from a seat in the back and joined him. "Why, that bitch," I murmured as Ann Burge leaned close to Williams, smiling up at him.

Ben turned, too. "Look at that."

"I'm surprised she came. Her mother lives in my neighborhood, and the old lady is adamantly opposed to the road construction."

Ben snorted. "Her daughter apparently isn't opposed at all." He turned back to face the new speaker.

I watched Ann Burge wrap herself around the stranger's right arm until they appeared joined at the hip. I stifled the surge of jealousy I felt at the sight of Ann, forty-ish, long-legged and slender with flowing dark red hair and a killer figure and killer fashion sense. Her blue linen slacks and matching striped blouse were casually chic, making her seem like she'd just stepped off a yacht for a chat with the peons. She and the guy were a matched set, like one of those magazine ads where people posed holding champagne glasses.

He paused in the doorway. Ann was speaking to him, her face upraised to his. He stared past her, and our eyes met. One side of his mouth quirked up in a sardonic smile, and he nodded once, then left, Ann clinging to him like a limpet.

I turned to the front again and focused on our new speaker. If Mr. Collins didn't show up, we would all have to expand our speeches to fill in for him. I began to mentally prepare myself, pulling my notepad from my bag to make a checklist of items. As I did, the letters I retrieved from my mail box fell out and scattered. "Damn," I muttered, bending over to get them. One slid along the polished wooden floor, and I had to get down on my hands and knees to find it.

I managed to get back onto my chair with my dignity intact and smoothed my skirt, letters clutched in my right hand. I was putting them back into my bag when one caught my attention. It had no stamp or address on it, only my name in a thin and elegant black calligraphy, with the first initials of my name, the J and the A, twice as tall as the rest.

I turned it over and that's when I saw it wasn't sealed. The flap was tucked into the envelope. Intrigued, I removed a folded piece of heavy ivory notepaper, like the kind used for invitations. My name was once again written on the flap. I opened it and at first wasn't sure what I was seeing. The handwriting was full of swoops and swirls and curlicues, so much so it was difficult to see the smaller bases of each letter.

I blinked a few times and finally could decipher the elegant missive.

Miss Austin:

I know you to be a woman of integrity and courage, so I trust you with this knowledge. I fear for my life, and the local police decline to aid me in any way. In fact, I am unsure if I can even trust the police because I fear they may be a part of the conspiracy that threatens me.

If I should meet with an "accident," please don't allow my death to go unremarked. My opposition to the road construction project has uncovered some very unsavory practices on the part of the local college, land owners, and officials. They will stop at nothing to get what they want. A large amount of money is at stake, and the greed of some people knows no bounds. I am seeking legal advice on how to proceed, but I fear I may not be able to act in time.

I have secured copies of important documents in a safe place, known only to me and an acquaintance who once was a friend. Sometimes the old ways are the best ways. The hiding place was used often in the past and went unremarked, and I trust it will do so again.

Remember this letter in the event of my death.

S. Collins

I stared down at the oddly worded note. What was he talking about? It sounded like something in a Victorian novel. Not trust the police? Granted, our small police force didn't have much experience, but surely they weren't corrupt, as he implied. And why would the old man be in fear for his life? What kind of unsavory practices did he uncover?

And perhaps most importantly: why the hell was he getting me involved in his paranoia?

I read the note again then folded it and put it back into my bag with the other mail. There was nothing I could do about it now and talking to Mr. Collins would just have to wait until the meeting finished. I tuned in to the county engineer, a portly man who spoke in short bursts, emphasizing his words with brisk taps on the podium. He expounded on the history of the Manortown Extension, as the road project was known, extolling its virtues. It would connect the nearby college town of Manortown where Derby College was located to Longbarn via a four-lane highway extension to an existing sleepy country road.

The extension was just south of the fen near my

home, and if the construction was approved, it would go smack through the wildlife refuge which was home to an endangered species of turtle. The Sierra Club, various wildlife groups, and a several dozen concerned citizens, myself included, had organized to prevent the extension from taking place. We were being slowly worn down, though, by time and money. The proposal was drafted ten years ago when there was no Federal funding. But in the last year, the wealthy donors at the private college swayed a new legislature to their plan to add a new highway extension to bring more traffic to their town.

The fact that the extension would lay waste to delicate marsh lands and put a wildlife refuge in danger did not deter its supporters. This town meeting was a chance to hear arguments pro and con for the project before it was submitted for final approval.

"What's going on?" Ben leaned forward to peer past me.

"What? Where?" I turned to my right.

Ann Burge and her mother stood in the doorway, Dr. Williams behind them. Mrs. Burge wore a pretty navy skirt with matching polka-dot blouse and a small navy hat. Her white hair was permed and swirled, and I was sure her makeup was tasteful and appropriate, as it always was. She looked like she was going to a garden party, as out of place with the casual crowd as a formal flower in a field of dandelions.

Mrs. Burge spied Ben and I and began hurrying across the crowded auditorium, moving spryly for a woman in her eighties. Several heads turned to watch her progress and to watch her daughter, who followed the old lady like a ship being towed. Williams watched them both from the doorway, glancing once at a large silver wristwatch.

Mrs. Burge finally reached us and leaned over me to speak to Ben. "The most terrible thing has happened," she said in a low voice, glancing from me to Ben then to the others in our group who sat nearby.

"Please, have a seat," I said, nudging Ben. "Move over." I was surprised to see the old woman at this display of civic discussion. She disapproved of the road project, but she never showed up at any of our meetings and never responded to any phone calls or letters we sent her. The fact that she was here might help our cause a great deal. The Burges were big names in the Longbarn community.

"No, that's fine. I thought you should know." The old lady shook her head sadly. "Mr. Collins is dead."

Chapter 2

I gaped at her. "Dead? How?"

"I'm not sure, but I saw the police at his house. When I went there to see what was happening, one of the officers, a rude young man, told me he was dead."

"Mother, I can't stay. We're going out for dinner." Ann tugged at her mother's arm, but the old lady shook her off.

"That's fine, Ann. Go on." Mrs. Burge glanced at the doorway, where Dr. Williams still waited. "You and your friend have an enjoyable time." Her tone of voice was so frosty I was surprised Ann didn't shiver.

"We were hoping you could join us," Ann said, undeterred by her mother's obvious displeasure.

"You know I have my bridge club tonight. I'll see you later." Mrs. Burge swept her daughter with a disdainful look, then focused her attention over my head, at Ben. "I realize Mr. Collins wanted to speak on behalf of your coalition, and I thought you should know he won't be here."

"I appreciate you taking the time to tell me," Ben said.

I huddled in my seat, letting them talk. I caught a glimpse of Ann Burge's face above me. Her mouth was set in a grim line, and bright spots of red color shone on her normally pale cheeks. She reminded me of one of those little flashing robots from my childhood, the kind that shot sparks as it walked. I got the impression she might ignite at any moment.

"We'll take a short recess then we have several speakers who have requested an opportunity to present an opposing view of this project," the mayor said, shooting us a disapproving glare.

"I'll talk to you later, Mother," Ann snapped then she wheeled and strode through the crowd that was getting to its feet, taking a break.

"I'm sure you will," Mrs. Burge muttered. She glared at her daughter's retreating back then when she saw me watching her, she smiled perfunctorily. "Ann tends to over-worry about my ability to manage my life."

"A natural tendency in a daughter," I said tactfully. "It's so convenient she lives near you, isn't it?" Ann's house was west of Collins', with one house between them. Her parents built her the house when she married years earlier, and she got the house in the divorce.

"Convenient is not how I would describe it." Mrs. Burge stared down at me, her gaze flickering over my denim skirt and sweater, correctly assessing my couture as JC Penney. "I read a review of your novel. Dr. Williams is a friend of Ann's. He's new here. I suppose he didn't know you lived in town."

I was equally sure Dr. Williams knew I was a local. If nothing else, the people at the newspaper office would have told him because they knew me. "It shouldn't matter if I'm from here or not. He's entitled to his opinion."

"Pity it was so negative."

I heard nothing of pity in her voice, but I smiled anyway. "Yes, but you know what they say. The only bad publicity is no publicity. I'm sure it will help sales if only to pique the curiosity of those who read the review."

"Perhaps." The old biddy invested a world of doubt in the single word. "Well, I've done my neighborly duty and let you know about Mr. Collins." She turned to leave, but several people were standing in the aisle near our seats and she had to angle her way around them to get away. The sour expression on her face clearly told me what she thought of this hoi polloi milling about. I watched her walk sedately from the room, her head held high.

"Did you see anything unusual when you stopped at his house?" Ben asked. "Did you see any sign of him?"

I shook my head. "None. I walked to the back, but I didn't see anyone. I didn't go to the fen, but I could see that the walkways were still above water."

"I wonder what happened," Ben said. "Maybe it was a heart attack."

"Would the police be there for a heart attack? Wouldn't that be a matter for the ambulance? Although I suppose when the ambulance is called, the police need to show up. I wonder who found him. I mean, who called the police?"

Ben's dark eyes were sympathetic. "Maybe he heard you knock on his door but he couldn't answer. Or maybe he called the police."

Such a grim thought. What if the poor man was lying there while I was prying about, wandering around his property. I thought of the note in my bag. I considered showing it to Ben then decided I should show it to the police. But should I? The note implied that the police might not be trustworthy. It might just offend them. Although I suppose police were trained not to be offended when people didn't trust them.

And let's face it. The note was hardly evidence of anything. It wasn't like I *had* to show it to the police. It wasn't like the note held anything pertinent to his death. Mr. Collins didn't directly implicate a specific person.

Implicate? What was I saying? The poor old man probably had an accident or a heart attack. There was nothing to imply that foul play was involved.

"I was counting on Mr. Collins to give a history of the property," Ben said worriedly, fumbling with a notebook that contained his "strategy" papers.

I was happy to have my thoughts diverted from their dire path. "Do you have information about it? Maybe I can add it to my talk."

"Would you? That would be great. Mr. Collins was going to do an overview of the history of the area. Joe from the Sierra Club is tackling the environmental aspects, I'm covering economic, and you were discussing the neighborhood impact. But if you could work in the history, that would be perfect."

I extended my hand. "Let me skim your notes and I'll see what I can do."

He took a sheaf of papers from the notebook and shuffled through them. "His family settled the land back in the 1800s, so he's got a lot of details about land use. Did you know that the Collins family and the Burge family had a feud going?"

"What kind of feud?" I extracted my small spiral notebook from my bag to go through my notes. I had decorated the notebook with pictures of the endangered turtle and pictures of the flowers in the marsh. I always decorated my notebooks with whatever was pertinent to the subject matter within.

Ben handed several sheets of notebook paper to me, and I glanced through them. Thank heavens. Someone had typed these notes so I didn't need to decipher Mr. Collins' ornate handwriting. "Apparently back in the war years—the big war, you know, World War II—someone in Mr. Collins' family jilted someone in Catherine Burge's family."

"Really? I didn't know they socialized." I scanned the list of dates and details.

"I think the Burges are only recently wealthy."

"They don't act that way. They act like they're landed gentry and the rest of us are encroaching on their property by breathing their air."

Ben hurriedly reassembled his notebook before papers started to unhinge themselves. "Not at all. I spent a lot of time talking with Mr. Collins when we started our organization. From what I gathered from him and from his notes, the Burges came into a lot of money in the 1940s or 50s. They built their house first then they started to sell off pieces of property. Mr. Collins' father insisted he owned land, but the Burges claimed it, too. There were different surveyors brought in, and that ended up in court. Mr. Collins said it cost his father a fortune. He's very bitter about that." Ben's bushy eyebrows drew together in a sad frown. "I mean, he was very bitter."

"I had no idea." Actually, I was barely listening. I was desperately skimming through seven pages of notes replete with dates, scribbles, cryptic comments, and abbreviations.

"From what he told me, the Burges made a bundle

when they sold the land for housing then they brought in their own developers who were family members and made a double killing when they built houses and sold them. Mr. Collins and his family were left with a few acres near the marshland."

"That doesn't sound fair," I murmured, jotting dates and events in the margins of my notes concerning the neighborhood.

"Apparently back in the 1940s and 1950s when the neighborhood was established, the town didn't really pay attention to what was going on. I mean, Longbarn was still just a village back then. And your neighborhood was on the outskirts of town."

"And now Longbarn is a bustling metropolis of twenty-thousand people and the town is trying to finally bring my neighborhood into its boundaries." I glanced at Ben but he wasn't paying attention to me. He had returned to staring at his notes so hard I thought he'd bore a hole through the paper.

I gave up on making conversation and focused on studying my own jottings. Too soon our brief break was over and the mayor called the meeting back to order. "Our first speaker represents the Sierra Club, which has requested an environmental review of this project. Then members of a group in town who are organized in opposition wish to speak. This group—" He fumbled for the papers on his desk.

I stood. "SOFT. Save Our Fen Turtles. We're a grass-roots community organization. Several hundred citizens have joined us."

The mayor glared at me. "They've circulated a petition and have—"

"I'm sorry to interrupt," I said. "But we plan to

discuss that during our talk. Ben and I will speak for the members of our group."

I thought the mayor might declare me in contempt of court. "Please proceed," he said to the Sierra Club rep. "Each speaker is limited to ten minutes."

The man took his place at the podium and delivered a clear, concise evaluation of what the construction would do. He showed several excellent slides of the flora and fauna at the site that would be displaced.

"What is the cost of progress?" he asked in summation, showing slides of different extinct species. "It's true that extinction is possible even without humans causing it, but this is one case where humans will be directly involved in the extinction of a species."

I saw the county engineer sit up in his seat as though he'd stand. The Sierra Club guy saw it, too, and he said, "Despite the assurances of the planning commission and the county engineer, there is no way to build a four-lane highway through a delicate ecosystem and not have it impact the inhabitants. You may say that a turtle, a butterfly, and a small rose-like flower are not as important as giving citizens a chance to move faster from point A to point B. But ask yourselves this question: will your children agree with you?"

He sat down amid a buzz of conversation. "You're next," Ben murmured.

I stepped into the aisle and approached the podium, nodding to the mayor and the members of the city council when I passed them. I adjusted the microphone downward for me so I didn't have to stand on my tiptoes.

"Please state your name, occupation, and place of

residence," the mayor said, jotting notes on a pad in front of him.

"Jane Austin, spelled with an 'i'. I'm a teacher and a writer. I live on Rosings Drive, a mile or two west of town."

Mrs. Gardiner, one of the council people, smiled at me. "I read your book. Well done. I enjoyed it thoroughly."

Mrs. Bennet, another councilwoman, glared at her. "We're not here to discuss literature. We're here to discuss progress."

"That's the matter that's up for debate, isn't it?" I retorted. "Whether this road is necessary for progress and if it is, at what cost? I live not far from where the road will go and I am concerned about the impact it will have on my neighborhood. But the greater concern is the impact it has on our region as a whole. You've heard from the environmentalists about that, but let me tell you about the impact on me, someone who is an ordinary citizen like you."

I launched into a description of my bucolic neighborhood, interspersing snippets of facts about when the land was settled, farmed, and finally subdivided. As I was talking, I spied Ann Burge enter with Dr. Williams. They took seats near the door, causing a ripple effect when people had to move to make room for them.

"While I appreciate the fact that a mere handful of turtles may not seem an adequate reason to halt this project, I ask that you consider the larger implications." Williams smiled condescendingly at my use of his phrasing. I skewered him with a glare in return. "This marsh and fen area are home not only to the endangered

Blandings turtle, but to several species of butterflies and several plants. If we allow this project to continue, we will upset the delicate balance not only of the marsh, but of the neighborhoods that adjoin it."

I stared directly at the smug gentleman sitting at the back of the room. "I know that I may not be a completely objective speaker on this because I have a vested interest in the outcome of these discussions. This isn't just a case of NIMBY or 'Not In My Back Yard'. That's only one facet of this disturbing forward march of so-called progress. We need to weigh the benefits and the detriments to all landowners, not only the college and the people associated with it, but to the residents who have lived for so long near the path of the road. We must find a balance for ourselves and for the future."

I stepped back from the podium and returned to my chair, smiling at the few congratulatory murmurs that came to me from the spectators. When I took my seat, I glanced at Ann and her date. She stared frostily at me, but he smiled, as if her anger amused him. I decided there and then that he was an arrogant idiot.

Ben rose and took his place at the podium, notebook tucked under his arm and his plain face set with a determined look. He didn't have much adjusting to do to the microphone because he was slightly taller than me.

I had helped him rehearse his speech a couple of times, so I listened only partially to what he said. Most of my mind was consumed with the news about Mr. Collins. It was certainly odd that I got a letter like that from him just before his death. Why would he send such a note to me? He and I weren't friends. We were simply acquaintances who were united in a common cause. I seldom saw him in the neighborhood and when I did, the only acknowledgement we made of each other was a brief wave and an occasional chat.

Why would he think I was a 'woman of courage and integrity'? I moved into the neighborhood ten years earlier, after the scandal that ejected me from Derby College. Was he referring to that old gossip? I suppose it was possible he heard what happened. The administration at Derby tried to hush it up, but rumors inevitably leaked out.

I acted then with what I hoped was integrity, but it did cost me my job. Luckily the administration at the local community college did a fair job of investigating my background and they concluded I wasn't a threat to their students and they hired me. Perhaps Mr. Collins heard about it. Our neighborhood wasn't a great one for socializing. One and two acre lots preclude any neighborly get-togethers. But gossip does make the rounds and I didn't doubt that he might have gotten at least one view of what happened.

I tuned in to Ben's speech and realized he was wrapping up. I began to gather my papers together, and the printed sheets Ben gave me caught my eye. The dates and events associated with them felt incorrect somehow, but I couldn't put my finger on what was wrong. Land bought, land worked, deeds registered, houses built, roads installed, roads named, subdivisions created.

I puzzled over the list for a few seconds, but whatever was bothering me wasn't immediately obvious. I tucked the sheets into my book bag, resolving to copy them and return them to Ben later.

"I want to thank the people who took the time to prepare for this meeting and who gave their time to present their opinions." The mayor fixed the restive audience with a quelling stare. "The council will take the opinions under advisement, and further public meetings will be held before final funding is considered for this project. Thank you for attending."

That was the signal for people to head for the exits. Ben and I gathered our things and joined the others meandering toward the doorway, pausing now and again to chat with those who wanted more details about our talks. Because of that, it was fifteen minutes after the first people started to leave before he and I were at the exit.

Joan Murray, editor-in-chief and publisher of the *Barn and Bugle*, was waiting for me inside the doors near the exit. She was a skinny, tanned woman whose two loves were the newspaper and golf. Her unruly short blonde hair was already showing sun streaks and it was only June. By August her hair would be white from her hours in the sun. As always, she wore dark blue Bermuda shorts and a pale blue golf shirt, her standard attire from May to October. The only variation was the color combinations and whether or not she wore sandals or sneakers. "Jane, do you have a minute?" she asked.

Ben was stopped off to one side, chatting with a group of people. "I need to talk to Joan," I told him. "I'll see you tomorrow night, okay?"

He gave a short wave. "See you later."

Joan pulled me aside, near where Ann Burge and her date sat earlier. They were nowhere in sight now. "I wanted to apologize for that book review. I didn't check it before it was sent in for typesetting."

"Don't worry about it." I touched Joan's arm reassuringly. She was about ten years younger than me, but she worried so much about her newspaper that she seemed at least a decade older. "He's entitled to his opinion. And let's face it. I'm sure I'll get bad reviews, so I may as well get it out of the way now."

"I'm glad you feel that way. You won't hold it against us? You'll still write your column?" She regarded me anxiously, her pale blue eyes wide with worry.

"Of course I'll keep writing my column. I'm just putting the finishing touches on the one for next week." Joan was so relieved I put an arm around her and gave her a quick hug. "You worry too much."

"I suppose I do, but it was such a nasty review."

"You know..." A germ of an idea began to percolate in my brain. "You should have him do a review of my column."

"Your column? The Nature Girl stories?"

I nodded. I wrote a monthly column for the paper under the pseudonym Nature Girl. They were short, humorous, and well-loved by the public. Nature Girl got all kinds of mail from the readership. "That might be interesting, to see what he says about the author of Nature Girl versus the person who wrote *The Gentleman and the Lady.*"

Joan began to smile, her un-lipsticked mouth quirking up on the right. A mini-stroke two years ago left some of Joan's facial muscles fixed, so it often appeared as though she was smirking. "I like the idea," she mused. "Maybe I could ask him to review a few of our columnists, so I don't single yours out. You know, ask for the outsider viewpoint on our small-town newspaper. Maybe nothing for publication, but just to get his professional evaluation."

Something in her tone of voice alerted me. "Is he a bit snobbish?"

"A bit?" Joan shook her head. "He suggested he should review a real novel, not a genre novel. Something from Oprah's book club." She hooked her fingers in the air around *real*.

"Yeah, like a romance novel doesn't count." I was familiar with that viewpoint among various writing groups, especially those at the college. "Where did you find him? I mean, did someone recommend him? Did he approach you?"

Joan grimaced. "Derby College's president called me and suggested him. Apparently, he's new and the president thought it might be good for him to get involved with the community."

I grinned. "He's involved, all right. He spoke tonight at the meeting."

"Really? In favor of the road, I suppose." She shot an angry glare at the council members who were still at the front of the auditorium, talking. "Everybody acts like it's a done deal. I can't believe they're ramming a road through a wildlife refuge."

"It's not a done deal yet," I said. "The environmental impact study has to be evaluated by the federal government before they'll allocate any funding for it. Hopefully someone there will recognize what a mistake it is." I started for the exit and Joan fell into step with me. "I'll keep fighting it to my dying day. That reminds me. Did you hear that Mr. Collins died? The old man who lived down the street from me?"

She nodded. "The report came in on the police scanner. Someone found him in the fen. He'd fallen off the walkway and drowned. Or—" She frowned. "Now that I think of it, there wasn't a specific cause of death mentioned. I just assumed. I should check that. They took the body to the Medical Examiner's office."

"Medical Examiner?"

"I think they do an autopsy when it's not obviously natural causes." Joan glanced at her watch. "If I hurry, I might be able to catch a friend of mine who works at the hospital. Maybe she's heard something. You're sure you're not pissed off about the review?"

"I'm sure," I assured her. We walked into the lobby, passing two police officers. The presence of the police wasn't surprising since the police station was in the building adjacent to city hall. As we walked past, one of the officers stepped forward.

"Miss Austin?"

Joan and I halted. "Yes?"

"Could we have a word with you?" He was young, with an unlined face and crew cut blond hair. His partner was older, a stocky man who watched people walk past us, his gaze bouncing from person to person.

I glanced at Joan. "Go. Get your news story. I'll drop the article off at the office in the morning."

Her gaze swiveled from me to the officers. "You're sure?"

"Of course. Go on." I turned to the police officer. "How can I help you?"

Joan hurried away, joining with the last of the spectators leaving the auditorium. The police officer walked back to his partner, and I followed.

"We'd appreciate it if you could come to the

station to answer a few questions." It wasn't phrased as a request.

"About what?" I glanced at the clock over the exit doors. It was eight-thirty and I had a class to teach in the morning.

"What do you know about the death of Samuel Collins?" The younger cop moved to my right. I automatically shifted position, ending up between him and his partner.

"Mr. Collins' death? Nothing. I just heard about it tonight." I looked at the older partner, but his attention was on our surroundings, as though expecting someone to do something illegal at any time.

"Are you sure?" the younger one persisted.

"Of course, I'm sure. Why?"

"You were the last person to see him alive."

"What? I haven't seen him for a day or two. Who told you that?"

"Miss Burge said that you were at the Collins house this afternoon."

"Indeed, I was," I said. "I didn't see Miss Burge, though."

"She was at her mother's house. She saw your car and she saw you walking around the house. What did you see?"

"Let's go back to the station," the older partner said. "No need to stand here and talk."

It was not an invitation. I considered balking, but I wasn't sure that was wise. I had nothing to hide and maybe if I chatted with them, the whole thing could be resolved in a few minutes. "Of course," I said. "My car is just outside. I'll drive over there and meet you."

"We'll walk," the officer said. "Don't worry. We'll

make sure you have an escort back here to get your car." He turned, and so did his partner, effectively blocking me in and herding me toward a side door.

I decided not to worry about this minor show of police force and instead use it to my advantage. "How did Mr. Collins die?" I asked as the two men ushered me from the building.

"We'll discuss it when we get to the police station." The younger man put a hand on my arm to propel me out the door.

"Now just a minute." I stood my ground, jerking my arm away from him. "I am happy to cooperate, but I will not be manhandled like a criminal. I've done nothing except attempt to verify the well-being of my neighbor. I do not deserve to be treated like I'm guilty of some crime." I crossed my arms and glared at them.

"Is something wrong, Jane? Is there anything I can do to help?"

I turned and found George Wick approaching us from the auditorium. "What are you doing here, George?" I doubted he was here from any sense of civic duty.

"I was hoping to talk to Ben. Is there a problem here, officers?" George smiled affably at the two men.

"Miss Austin apparently doesn't want to be interviewed concerning her involvement in the death of Mr. Samuel Collins," the younger one said.

The older one closed his eyes briefly, and I think he was praying for patience. "We wanted to chat with Miss Austin about her visit to Mr. Collins' house," he said to George. "We thought it would be more comfortable and more private to talk at the station."

"About what?" George stood next to me, and I

confess it felt good to have him there. He was a tall, slender man with an engaging, boyish air despite the flecks of gray in his thick brown hair. George wasn't handsome, but he was appealing in a puppy-dog sort of way. He turned to me. "Jane, do you know anything about Mr. Collins' death?"

I shook my head. "No, I went to his house this afternoon to try to talk to him, but I didn't see him there."

"Talk to him about what?" the younger officer demanded.

"He was supposed to speak at tonight's meeting but no one on the committee had spoken to him today. I live near him, so I volunteered to stop by his house and make sure he was okay. But I didn't see him when I was there, and no one answered the doorbell, so I came here to speak at the meeting."

The older officer hooked his thumbs in the big utility belt around his waist. "It appears we were misinformed. We were led to believe you and he talked together this afternoon."

"I haven't seen him since yesterday," I said. "We chatted briefly at the grocery store."

"So you see, officers, it's a misunderstanding." George pulled a small leather case from his back pants pocket and extracted two business cards. "If there are any further questions, don't hesitate to contact me at the same time you contact Miss Austin. I'm her attorney, so of course I'll need to be present for any conversation you may have with her." He handed the cards to the officers then put his hand gently under my elbow. "Let's go, Jane."

The younger officer glanced at the business card.

"Thank you, Mr. Wick. We'll be in touch if we need any information."

George steered me away, back through the main lobby.

"How did you do that?" I whispered as we sauntered away. "I thought they were going to lock me up."

George flashed perfect white teeth at me. "It's a gift. You simply have to imagine what the other people feel then figure a way to make them feel better. What is truly interesting, though, is why they're concerned about Mr. Collins' death. When I first heard about it, I assumed he had a heart attack."

We were nearing the exit doors and once again, I put on the brakes. "You heard about it already?"

George pushed open the door for me. "Mrs. Burge told her bridge club. You know what a gossipy old crew that is. Mrs. Somebody called her daughter, who called someone, who was talking to Lydia, and she told me."

We stepped into the cool night air, and I walked through the now empty parking lot to my car. "I don't understand why the police think I might have anything to do with it," I said.

"They don't, not really. It's just their job. Speaking of which…" He leaned on my car, watching me open the door. "It seems like you just hired me as your lawyer. Should we discuss a fee?" I opened the door and leaned to put my book bag on the passenger seat. George intercepted me and tugged me close to him. "I don't mind taking payment in trade," he murmured before jerking me hard against him.

Chapter 3

I managed to get one arm free, then I pushed George as hard as I could. "You're a married man," I said while he tried to catch his balance. "You should be ashamed of yourself."

He laughed. "Lydia and I have an understanding. Don't be so old-fashioned."

"You and she may have an understanding, but you and I don't." I slipped into the car before he could make another attempt.

"Are you worried about your reputation? Don't be. No one in town cares what we do. Don't be such a prude, Jane." George leaned over my open door.

"Back off, George, or I'll slam this door on your hand." I don't know what angered me most—that he was betraying his marriage vows or that he was hitting on me to do so. Either way I was mad as hell.

"No need to be so upset. I'll still represent you," he called after me when I gunned the motor and drove away.

I shot out of my parking space but had the presence of mind to slow when I neared the exit. As I did, I passed Dr. Williams and Ann Burge, who stood next to a silver BMW sports sedan. They both watched me drive past and Williams looked back at George, whom I saw watching me in my rear-view mirror.

"Oh, great," I muttered. "Now that old gossip will

be resurrected just because Ann Burge saw George Wicks making a pass at me. Damn it all." I fumed all the way back to my house and was still fuming when my phone rang.

"Do you want me to shoot that reviewer for you?" a bantering voice said. "I can do it, you know. I'm a crack shot."

I poured myself a glass of wine with the phone balanced against my collarbone. "Thanks, Fran. Tell me, how can such a miserable human being be so handsome?"

"Hey, don't ask me. You know my gate doesn't swing that way. I'm not the woman to ask about male beauty." Franny Benton laughed. She was one of my best friends and the unofficial leader of the Bossy Posse, my group of seven female friends of varying ages who critiqued my novels and encouraged me on my road to publication. "Did you meet him?"

I wandered out to my porch and sank down on my wicker couch. "He spoke at the meeting tonight." I peered into the darkness, the only lights those from Mrs. Burge's house in the distance. "Mr. Collins died today. Or at least, they found his body today. The police are investigating it."

"I already heard. Old Lady King called Edie who called Cassie who told me. Mrs. King heard it from Mrs. Burge at bridge club tonight. And then Jamie called and said she talked to Charlie who said her nephew who works at the hospital said that Doc Lucas was called in because he had to examine the body."

"Good Lord. George was right. There are no secrets in this town."

"George?"

I sipped my wine, trying to wash away my anger. "George Wick. I ran into him at the town meeting." I tried to think of some way to briefly summarize my confrontation with the police and George's intervention and decided it just wasn't worth the time or effort. "Anyway, there's apparently some kind of question about how Mr. Collins died. The police are interested."

"He was knifed. That's what I heard."

"Holy buckets, are you serious?" I choked on the wine I was swallowing.

"Either that or strangled. I heard it was something violent." Fran sounded remarkably complacent about such a horrible death. Of course, she didn't know Mr. Collins so she had no interest in his demise, but she still sounded blasé.

"I wonder if I have anything to be nervous about." Even as I said it, I noticed how very dark it was around my house, how isolated I was, and that a man was presumably murdered a half-mile away from me. I hurriedly went back inside the house and locked the porch door behind me. "Well, I'm sure the police will work out what happened."

"Yeah, right. Anyway, that's not why I called. I wanted to see if you needed me to bring anything besides my famous mini-wienies on Saturday."

"I think we'll have enough food. I'm making queso blanco to go with chips, Charlie and Edie are bringing veggies, Hank and Jamie are bringing a shrimp platter, Cassie said she'd bring humus and pita, and Georgie is bringing bread and artichoke dip. I think the Bossy Posse has it covered. I've got wine in a box, lots of different beer, some pop, and a washtub in the garage to fill with ice. I'd say that's a party waiting to happen."

"Well, if you need anything at the last minute, just holler. Cassie and I will get there early and help set up."

I knew it would be useless to protest. Franny and her sister Cassie were both retired and they partied at the drop of a hat. My book launch celebration was the highlight of June for them. "Thanks, I'm sure I'll need it. Listen, I have to go. I've got classes tomorrow. Summer semester just started, and I need to get those kids kicked in the butt."

Franny laughed again. "Okay, we'll see you tomorrow. And don't forget to lock your doors tonight in case the boogie man is out."

I needed no reminding, but I still double-checked my doors and windows before bed.

The next day was Friday, which was one of my busy days this semester along with Monday and Wednesday. I had a nine o'clock a.m. Introduction to Business Communication class, an eleven o'clock a.m. Creative Writing class, and a one o'clock p.m. Social Literature class. The Soc Lit class was relatively new, a curriculum I designed to give aspiring business students an overview of classic literature in case they were ever called on to discuss it during a cocktail party or other social venue. My hope was they wouldn't be embarrassed mistaking Tequila Mockingbird for *To Kill a Mockingbird*.

I also had to polish my article for Tuesday's newspaper. My *Nature Girl* articles appeared on the third Tuesday of each month. This month's article, *Nature Girl Defends the Gold Fish,* chronicled my tussle with a snake in my small pond in the back yard. Joan Murray, my editor, wanted me to expand it so I needed to embellish the tale slightly.

I spent the morning in class or talking with students and part of the afternoon in my miniscule office at the community college. Consequently, it was nearly three o'clock before I left, dropping by the grocery store to pick up last-minute supplies and getting to my house at four o'clock. I spent the remainder of the evening working on student papers and spent most of Saturday cleaning and getting ready for my party.

At four o'clock I quickly changed clothes into royal blue capris with a matching polka-dot blouse and my comfortable blue sandals. Then I lured Persuasion into the bedroom with kitty treats and made sure he was comfortable for the evening. He was a sociable cat, but people would be coming and going. I didn't want to risk his escape.

The Bossy Posse began arriving at five o'clock. Franny and Cassie bustled into the kitchen, twin sixty-year-old dynamos. Cassie's husband Bill followed them carrying a box with a crockpot and several containers. Jamie and her wife Henrietta, a.k.a., Hank, arrived next and jostled for position with the others in my small kitchen. They were in my yoga class, which was how we met.

Georgie arrived next, stylishly dressed as always in a pretty flowered summer frock. She was a fifty-something widow with haute fashion sense and equally haute stilettos that made my feet ache just to see them. Last to arrive was the other couple in our group, Charlene and Edie, who taught at the community college in the Landscaping department.

I left the setup of the snacks to them and began greeting guests when they arrived. I invited everyone from the newspaper office, many of the faculty from the community college, a few old friends from Derby College, and my neighbors. By six-thirty my small house was overflowing with people. Lawn chairs were set up in the driveway on the north side and thus shaded from the setting sun. Guests helped themselves to beverages in the garage and food in the house and soon a party was underway.

As dusk was settling in, I glimpsed Ben and Charlotte Bing on the back lawn chatting with Mrs. Burge, who had commandeered my favorite chair near my pond and appeared to be holding court. I walked through the porch to join them and as I did Dr. Williams and Ann Burge came through the back door of my garage with drinks in hand. I hesitated, not anxious to butt heads with him, but I was too late. They saw me and changed direction.

Like the day before, they were twin ads from *Vanity Fair* or *Town and Country*. She wore a sleeveless pale green summer top, lightweight and shimmery with crisply ironed white capris. Her chunky sandals were tall enough to make her the same height as Williams, who wore dark jeans, a patterned blue shirt with sleeves rolled up and a dark blue vest. Both were casually elegant, stylishly informal.

"Thank you for inviting me, Jane," Ann said, her arm linked through Williams' to tug him forward to meet me. "I don't know if you've met Dr. Williams. Fitz, this is Jane Austin, our local romance author." With those four words and her tone of voice, she cavalierly dismissed my three-book contract with a major publishing house as inconsequential.

"Good to meet you," I said, taking his outstretched hand. "We should sit and chat sometime about the merits of using literary critiques for genre fiction. There are certain tropes in genre that are well accepted and often a critic needs to be aware of those in order to do an adequate review. It can be difficult to stay current with popular fiction, of course, when a person is entrenched in academe." I smiled, giving his hand a brisk shake. "That's one of the problems with tenure-track positions. Often a person becomes mired in what's well-known and finds it difficult to examine things outside a known purview."

Williams raised one dark eyebrow at my genial criticism. "I'd enjoy that discussion very much. I hope you didn't take offense at my review."

I waved a hand airily. "Not at all. Reviews, good and bad, come with being published. Just one of the perils of being the local romance author. You're new to town, aren't you?" I began walking across the lawn to Ben and the others, anxious to detach myself from these bothersome people.

"Yes, I moved here last year." He raised his plastic wine glass toward Charlotte, who stood with Ben a few yards away. Williams' other arm was supporting Ann while she tottered on the uneven grass. "Charlotte and I are old friends and she suggested me for the job when Dr. Knight passed away." His gaze went to my yard. "You have a lovely garden."

"Thank you," I said. "It's a hobby of mine. I enjoy gardening."

"So do I. I see you also use a sand bucket for your tools." He nodded toward the large metal pail near the garage. "Do you find it helps keep your tools clean?"

I was surprised he noticed it. "Yes, I use that when I don't have time to clean them."

"I add a touch of motor oil to mine," he said. "It helps keep the blades water repellant."

"I haven't tried that," I admitted.

"And now Fitz will be here full-time," Ann said, yanking the subject away from a topic she knew nothing about. Her flower beds were tended by a garden service and were minimal at best. "The school renewed his contract for the upcoming year."

I fought to keep my jealousy under control. Trust the damn college to get an outsider to fill a position I was perfectly capable of filling. I smiled so brightly I'm sure I appeared manic. "How exciting. I'm sure you'll fit right in at Derby. It's such an edifying institution."

"Jane used to teach at Derby," Ann explained with a smirk that ended in a small gasp when her ankle twisted.

Williams turned to help her and missed the baleful glare I shot Ann. "Yes, I did. Now I teach at the Community College. And write romance novels on the side. If you'll excuse me, I need to chat with some other guests. Good to meet you." I left before Williams or Ann could sling any more barbs at me.

I greeted Mrs. Burge, who nodded imperiously at me then I went to Ben and Charlotte. "Thanks for coming. You help balance the excess snobbery in the air."

Charlotte laughed. She was a tall, big-boned woman with curly blonde hair, wide blue eyes, and a small mouth that appeared triangular when she smiled. What she lacked in appearance she made up for in personality. Charlotte and Ben were so perfectly matched. They were easy-going, down-to-earth people without a mean word to say about anyone.

"Give Fitz a chance," Charlotte said. "He's not as stuck-up as you think."

"He's with Ann," I pointed out. "I doubt anyone could give him a chance, if you know what I mean." I winked and turned to Ben. "How do you think it went yesterday? I wish Mr. Collins was there to speak. He could have provided some historical perspective on how the land was used."

"Have you heard anything more about his death?" Charlotte asked. "I heard the police are investigating."

"Nothing more. I was at his house yesterday, but I didn't see him." I glanced back at Ann Burge, who stood near her mother. The old woman appeared less than happy to have her daughter nearby. "Ann apparently saw me there and decided to rat on me to the cops. I had an uncomfortable moment or two with them yesterday until I convinced them I didn't see him when I was there."

"Seriously?" Charlotte looked past me. "What was she doing spying on her neighbors?"

I shrugged. "She lives nearby so I suppose she saw me poking around."

"Did you talk to his son?" Ben asked.

"When?" I saw members of the Bossy Posse circulating with appetizers and moved toward them, realizing I was shirking my hostess duties.

"He's here. He came to talk to you." Ben glanced at the people milling around the patio outside the porch. "There, in the plaid shirt. He introduced himself to me earlier."

"Thanks, I'll go talk to him. I didn't know he was here." I moved across the lawn but was intercepted by Dr. Williams, who left Ann standing next to Mrs.

Burge.

"I apologize if I offended you with my review." Williams sounded sincerely apologetic and looked very cute with his tousled gray hair and those big brown eyes. "Perhaps I was harsh in my criticism. I'm not accustomed to having such a small audience. No, wait, that didn't come out the way I meant." He smiled, shaking his head. "I'm making a mess of this, aren't I? I meant that I'm not accustomed to living in such a small community where what one says can be seen by just about everyone."

Now it was my turn to raise a supercilious eyebrow. "You're assuming that your review matters, Dr. Williams. Trust me. It doesn't matter to me, and I doubt it matters to anyone here." I raised a hand to encompass my guests. "You're entitled to your opinion about my genre, but I do take issue with your criticism about my abilities. I took great care to map out the arc for each character as well as the arc for the book and the series. The heroine's turning point was perfectly believable if you understood the nuances of the society of the time. As to the hero being—" I frowned at him, pursing my lips in thought. "Yes, you said he was rather spineless, I think. I thought I allowed his indecision to show rather nicely in the way he treated the secondary characters who were less fortunate than himself."

Williams blinked rapidly, struggling to keep pace with my rapid-fire delivery. "I confess I didn't evaluate the book in that light. Perhaps we could discuss—"

"I'm sorry. I need to talk with some other guests right now. You can call me at my office and perhaps we can meet for coffee and a discussion of literary structure and goal, motivation, and conflict in character development." I smiled and moved away. "You can find me in the Community College directory. Dr. Jane Austin."

His startled look was a sweet revenge for his condescending apology. I left Williams behind and hurried past my friends gathered around the fire pit where a low blaze was burning. I approached the tall man with shaggy brown hair speaking with Cassie. He was my age or maybe a bit younger, with a stocky build and an interesting face, craggy and rough, like a man who worked outside, perhaps.

"I'm so sorry for your loss," I said, extending my hand when Cassie moved away. "I'm Jane. Your father was a large part of our neighborhood. I often saw him when I took my walks, and he and I were involved in the turtle campaign, of course."

"I'm Luke Collins." He shook my hand. "It's good to meet you. We've been going through Dad's things, and he left some documentation that he wanted the committee to have. He had your name on some files."

"I'll be happy to help you however I can."

"Dad had planned to change his will when it became apparent the road project might go through. He talked about giving the land to the Sierra Club. They could fight the battle, not us." At that moment he was very like his father, his face pinching with dislike. "But he never did change it, and I don't know if I can cede the land to the Club since it's under contention."

"Contention? Really?"

"Can we go inside?" He nodded toward the house. "I don't like to say anything with them here."

"Them?"

He nodded toward the back yard. "The Burges.

You know about the lawsuit, right?"

"Do you mean the one from years ago?"

Luke stepped into the living room, shooting glances over his shoulder as though suspecting Ann Burge might follow. "No, the lawsuit going on now. My father was suing Mrs. Burge about the land."

"Good heavens, no, I didn't know." I was distracted by some guests who were leaving, and by the time I bid them farewell, I had lost my train of thought. "I'm sorry for the interruption," I told him. "Here, let's talk over here."

I ushered him into my study which was relatively private. People milled about outside on the porch on the east and in the hallway on the west, but the room itself was empty. "I didn't know your father was still involved in a lawsuit with the Burges. I was under the impression it ended years ago."

He shook his head, his thick brown hair brushing the collar of his faded blue plaid shirt. "No, it's been dragging on for years. Old Mrs. Burge won't let it go. She insists she owns all this land, but it's belonged to my father's family the whole time. Every time we think it might be resolved, she digs up some new witness or a document or something." He appeared as frustrated as he sounded.

"That must have been so stressful for your father," I murmured.

He glanced around my small study, but I doubt he really saw anything there. His mind was obviously elsewhere. "Dad really cared about the land. He loved that fen and the wildlife refuge. I swear he knew every inch of it. That's why it's so terrible that he should die that way."

"What way?" I blurted when he hesitated.

"He drowned. The police think he fell off the pathway." Luke paced my study, his empty, plastic glass dangling from his hand. "They're doing an autopsy, though."

"It's hard to believe your father would simply fall off the walkway," I said. "He was very careful whenever he went into the tricky parts. Everything is posted, too, with signs warning people about the bogs. That's just hard to believe."

"The police think he lost his balance. He was an elderly man, taking a walk and maybe he tripped or maybe he got dizzy." It sounded like he was trying to convince himself.

I spied my book bag, tossed on my armchair after last night's meeting. "Your father left me an odd note," I said, flipping open the bag's flap and pulling out yesterday's mail. "I don't know why he left it for me. I didn't know him very well." I thrust the note at Luke and took his empty glass from his hand, dropping the rest of the mail on my desk to deal with later.

He smiled as he read it. "This sounds so like Dad," he whispered. "He was always so dramatic. These last few years I swear he was getting a bit paranoid. The police told me he called them a couple of times about trespassers in the marsh." Luke shook his head. "Dad blamed Derby College for a lot of the problems. See what he says—the school landowners. Dad hated that Derby was in the business of owning property that was nowhere near their campus. He called them greedy landowners."

I peered over his shoulder at the note. "He says the school, landowners, and officials. Three different parties."

"I think that's a smudge, not a comma."

"It doesn't matter. But what does matter is that your father feared for his life." I took the note. "I think I should show this to the police."

"But he says he doesn't trust the police," Luke pointed out. "They'll just ignore you. After all, there's no proof that anything happened. Besides, no one would kill somebody because of a turtle."

"It's not just the turtle," I said. "There's a lot of money at stake. The land around the road can be developed if the road goes through. Right now, it's just wetlands and farmland and not very good farmland at that. Every spring a huge chunk of it floods. But if they put in a road, they'll build flood walls. The land will triple in value." I tapped the folded note against my palm for emphasis.

He didn't seem convinced. "Look at it this way. Why would someone kill my father? What would they gain?"

I frowned. "I'm not sure. But he was worried, and I feel I owe it to him to try to follow up on this." I wiggled the note. "I'll go to the police tomorrow and show it to them."

"I appreciate your concern, but I doubt they'll do anything. I'm willing to let the police handle everything. Speaking of handling things, I need to get going." He turned to the doorway.

"Will you be staying long?"

"I'll stay a few days but will come back when it's necessary and if I can get away. I own a ranch in Montana," he explained. "I have people who can watch it for me while I'm gone."

"Of course." I dropped the note on my desk near my plugged-in tablet computer.

"I'll drop off those papers tomorrow. Dad had everything organized and he made sure I understood what had to be done, so I know exactly where things are. I talked to his lawyer today and he said it was okay to start packing things."

It seemed rather indecently hasty to me, but I held my tongue. Different people handled grief in different ways. "Well, there's no rush on my part, but you do what works for you. If I'm not here, you can always leave anything on the porch." I gestured to my left, where people milled about on my side porch.

My glanced intersected that of Ann Burge, who stood immediately outside the open French doors. Her gaze was fixed on Luke Collins but when she saw me, she sauntered into the room as if she'd been invited. "Luke, it's good to see you again, although it's so sad, under the circumstances. I'm sorry for your loss." She advanced on him, hand outstretched. "Luke and I grew up together," she said to me as they shook hands. "He and I were the only children in this neighborhood growing up."

Luke released her hand quickly and nodded to me. "Thanks again. I'll drop by tomorrow."

"No rush," I assured him. "Whenever you can."

He hurried out, knocking into Ann in his haste. "Call me if you have time," she said.

Luke nodded and left. I smiled at his awkward haste until I realized that more than simple embarrassment fueled it. He honestly didn't want to stay in the same room with Ann longer than necessary.

She turned to me. "Luke and I went steady when we were younger. He left town when I broke up with him. This is the first time I've seen him since then." She swirled the red wine in her glass, peering at it thoughtfully. "He's still such a handsome man. It's terrible to think that because of me he and his father had such a bitter fight. This might be the first time Luke has been home in years. It's a pity he and his father didn't get along."

"That's odd. I didn't get that impression at all." I smiled sweetly at Ann's disbelieving expression. "We never know what goes on between a parent and a child, do we? Not everyone can have such a loving relationship, like you have with your mother."

Ann straightened. "My mother and I have an excellent relationship."

"I'm sure you do." My tone of voice conveyed my skepticism. "You're lucky she's in such fine health. I'm sure we'll have her with us for many more years to come."

Ann's lips thinned into a sour line. "Yes, we will, I'm sure. Unlike poor Mr. Collins." She moved past me, back to the French door.

"I didn't appreciate you lying to the police that I was the last person to see him alive."

She stopped in mid-step and turned slowly. "I beg your pardon?"

"You heard me." I glimpsed Dr. Williams behind her, poised to enter the study. When he saw Ann and me, he hesitated. I don't think she knew he was there.

"I was only doing my civic duty." She raised her pointed little chin, aiming it at me like a weapon.

"Bullshit. You've made my life a misery for years.

What did I ever do to deserve your attention?"

Ann stared at me, bright spots of color flaring to life on her pale cheeks. "I have no idea what you're talking about."

I stepped closer to her, pitching my voice low. "You caused my problems at Derby. You were sleeping with my husband and you cooked up that scheme that got me fired. I know all about it. Tommy told me before he left town. I think he was trying for some kind of last-ditch reunion with me by telling me how you masterminded the whole thing."

"That's ridiculous. Your ex-husband and I were friends. He often talked to me about his marital woes." One corner of Ann's mouth twisted up in a wry smile. "I was merely a sympathetic listener, that's all. He was starved for companionship."

I wanted to laugh. "Tommy Leroy never starved for companionship, believe me. When he was screwing you, he was screwing some student at the college. He might have been starved for my companionship because once I knew he was screwing around I refused to sleep with him. But Tommy always had a backup." I smiled. "Like you."

She went so rigid I thought she was having a stroke. Then she drew back haughtily, like I had an infectious disease. "All I did was report to the dean what I was told. How dare you accuse me of fabricating a lie?"

"I didn't accuse you of lying," I said. "I accused you of suborning an impressionable young man into lying. He was in your class, wasn't he? What did you threaten him with? Did you promise him a good grade if he did what you asked?" I frowned and tilted my head, supposedly in thought. I'd been waiting to say this to her for a decade and now that I had my chance, I would savor the moment. "Let's see, as I recall, he was failing your class. Then suddenly his grades improved." I stared into her eyes. "Maybe you were the one who was giving him that special attention, not me. He wasn't my student, after all. He was yours."

Ann drew in a deep breath, getting ready to blast me with her wrath. She stepped closer to me, but her shoe caught on the area rug and she twisted slightly. When she faced me again, she merely sighed instead of raging. "It's so sad that you won't admit the truth. You're so pitiable, Jane. You should learn from your mistakes, not try to sweep them under a rug." She set her plastic wine glass on my side table and turned to the French doors. "Oh, Fitz. There you are." She smiled at Dr. Williams and went to join him in the doorway. "Jane and I were just chatting."

"So I heard. Your mother was asking where you went. I think she'd like a ride home." Williams turned to me. "Thank you for your hospitality. I enjoyed myself."

"We can drop her off on the way to my house." Ann swept from the room, acting as regal as a queen. She stood on the porch, glaring at me.

I crossed my arms and glared right back at her. "She always gets the last word," I muttered. "Just once I'd like to beat her in an argument."

Williams took a step toward me. "I admire a woman who stands up for herself," he said in a low, confidential voice. "I've never been fond of victims. Well done, Miss Austin. Well done."

He left, leaning close to Ann to hear her

complaints. Just before they walked out of sight, he glanced back at me and winked.

Chapter 4

I didn't have time to consider Dr. Williams' enigmatic words. I had guests to mingle with and appetizers to hand out. A few hours later most of the guests were gone, which left Franny, Cassie, and Bill.

"Quite a successful party," Bill said while we puttered around the kitchen, cleaning up. Bill was a tall silver-haired retired banker who seemed to take everything in stride. I only saw him angry once, when a drunken snob started trash-talking about lesbians at the nearby country club. Bill stood up and told the manager he would be canceling his membership. The snob was ejected, and *his* membership was rescinded. "I will not tolerate demeaning talk about anyone based on their religion, sexual preference, or ethnicity," Bill told me later. "That's right up there with preying on the weak and taking advantage of those who can't fight back. I will not abide it."

"I'm glad so many people showed up," I said while I loaded the dishwasher. "I was surprised the Derby College contingent made an appearance. It's been years since I worked there. I don't see them very often."

"They're proud of you." Bill rinsed my dip dish and handed it to me. "You have a successful publishing career. Granted, it seems like every Tom and Joe is publishing a book nowadays, but you did it the old-fashioned way. You actually sold it to a publisher, and a rather well-known one at that."

"Well, when you put it that way," I said with a grin.

"I saw you talking to the cowboy." Cassie bustled into the kitchen, a tray full of plastic glasses in her hands. "He didn't seem too distressed about his father's death."

"What cowboy?" Franny asked, following behind her sister with another tray of glasses. "Recycle these?"

I pointed to the nearly overflowing blue bin. "Yep. Thank goodness the recycling guys come on Monday." I tucked the dip dish into the bottom rack of the dishwasher. "She means Luke Collins. I think he was upset about his father's death but not as upset as he should have been, if you know what I mean."

"Is he a real cowboy?" Franny demanded.

"He said he owns a ranch in Montana, so I guess he is."

"Everyone grieves in their own way," Cassie said. "After all, his father was elderly."

"The police say Mr. Collins fell off the walkway in the fen." I looked at my three friends expectantly.

"Not surprising," Bill said. "Perhaps he lost his balance. Did he drown?"

"I don't know." I turned to Franny. "You said he was strangled."

"That was the second rumor. The first one was that he was knifed. But now they're leaning toward accidental death, according to Charlie's nephew who works at the hospital. He apparently fell, hit his head, and drowned."

"His son didn't seem too upset about that," I commented. "Surely the police told him, right? And when I told him about the threatening note, he dismissed it as inconsequential."

"What threatening note?" Bill dried his hands on a dish towel.

"I'll show you. Hold on." I went into my study but didn't see the note where I left it. I rummaged on the desk, finally finding it under my computer tablet. I took it back to the kitchen and handed it to Franny. "Mr. Collins was concerned for his life. His son didn't seem to think it was important."

Franny stared at the note, Cassie peering over her shoulder. "What the hell is this, a foreign language or something?"

"It's cursive handwriting," Cassie said. "The kind of thing they don't teach to kids anymore. Let me see it."

"Hold on, hold on." Franny held the ornate note closer. "Okay, I got it now. Good heavens, he was a melodramatic old codger, wasn't he?" She handed the note to her sister and continued piling used plates and glasses into the recycling bin.

"Don't you see?" I insisted. "He knew someone was after him. He knew he was in danger."

Bill and Cassie read the note. "Interesting that he mentions the college land owners. I know that has peeved some of the alumni," Bill said. He was in on fund-raising efforts at Derby College in past years, so he knew a few of the more well-heeled alums.

"Luke said the same thing." I took the note from Cassie and stared at it. "I took it to mean the college and land owners, not the college which was a landowner."

"Like Dr. Williams?" Franny asked. "The

handsome stud muffin with Ann Burge? He's a landowner, isn't he? Didn't he buy some of the land south of here, along the river?"

"Is that who that was? He was cute. Pity he's with Ann. Wait a minute." Cassie shot me a suspicious look. "Is he that awful reviewer who thought your book was terrible? What was he doing here? He's lucky nobody knocked him out. If I'd known who he was, I would have given him a piece of my mind."

Bill put a hand on his wife's back. "Calm down, honey. Everybody's entitled to their own opinion, even if they are idiots."

"Unless they're an asshole," she snapped.

"Yes, he is the reviewer," I said. "Joan Murray told me she was kinda coerced into having him on the newspaper staff."

"That damn college," Franny muttered. "They've got their fingers into everything."

"I think I should talk to the police about the note." I put the note on the table in the kitchen nook. "Obviously Mr. Collins suspected his life was in danger. Perhaps he left more clues at his house." Then I remembered. "But his son said they're going through everything already. Important clues might be thrown out."

"According to that, the police are not to be trusted." Bill nodded at the note. "You might want to think twice about sharing that with them. It's possible the old man was a nuisance to them. You know how it goes. Our son in Missouri who's with the police says that they get calls all the time from people who are sure the neighbors are spying on them or sure there's a peeping Tom outside. They have to investigate, of course, but he said there are a few who are just chronic worriers. Maybe Mr. Collins was one of those."

"I'll think about it," I said. "He was a complainer. It seemed like he and Mrs. Burge had a feud going back decades. That reminds me. Did you know that Luke Collins and Ann Burge were once boyfriend and girlfriend, back when this was still farmland? When he saw her tonight, he ran like the devil was after him."

"Maybe there are some unpleasant memories there." Cassie turned, evaluating the now-tidy kitchen. "I think our job here is done, people. It was a lovely party. I'm so glad the weather cooperated." She hugged me, her small, round body soft against mine.

I went with them to the door and walked outside with them to their car. "What a beautiful night," I said, staring up at the star-studded sky. "You can see so many more stars here in the country."

Franny paused while getting in their car. "Not so much country anymore. Especially if that road goes through. You'll have a highway just a mile away."

I looked through the trees on my side lawn. From here I could glimpse the Collins house. Lights were on, glimmering through the trees. "It won't affect me too much, but it will surely annoy Mrs. Burge and Ann. I suppose Luke will sell the Collins house, but who would want to buy it? It's so close to the fen and the road if it goes through."

Cassie slipped into the front seat of the big sedan. "If there's a God, something will stop that road going through. We don't need another damn four-lane highway speeding people from place A to place B."

"Don't get your knickers in a knot. It isn't a done deal," Bill said, going around the car to the driver's side.

I stepped back while they pulled away from the curb. I walked into my front garden on the west side where my herbs were planted in a circular bed, several types of plants radiating from the center of lavender like spokes on a wheel. I sat on the small stump of cherry wood, salvaged from a tree cut down the past year. My resting place afforded me a clear view down the hill to the Burge house. Lights were on in the upstairs bedroom, but the rest of the house was dark. I knew it was midnight, but I saw a figure silhouetted in a window. I had the impression Mrs. Burge was eyeing my house. I'm sure she disapproved of the comings and goings so late at night.

I went into the house, locking the front door behind me and went to the back to let Persuasion loose from his isolation. He yawned and returned to sleep. I decided it was a good idea and joined him.

Thunderstorms woke me in the early morning, but I successfully ignored them and went back to sleep. When I got up at seven, a light drizzle was falling. The air was heavy and humid. Typical June weather in Iowa. I showered, dressed and went to the mailbox for my Sunday newspaper and the previous day's letters.

I took everything to my study and sorted through it, tossing junk mail into the recycle bin and leaving a few bills to be handled on my desk. I opened the bulky manila envelope from Thursday's mail and was preparing to pitch it into the recycle bin when I saw it wasn't a tedious legal document required by my investment manager, but was, instead, a brown accordion folder stuffed with documents.

I retrieved a few of the papers. They appeared old,

most of them slightly yellowed and faded. Contracts, letters, a title to a parcel of land, another title. It was a mishmash of documents, some personal some legal. Then I spied a letter in a distinctive, spidery handwriting, full of flourishes and curlicues.

It was from Mr. Collins to someone named George, dated forty years earlier. It was brief, almost brusque, and it read as if Collins was firing George or at least chastising him for some kind of dereliction of duty. It was very faded and smudged in spots, and it wasn't until I held it up to the light that I saw it was a carbon copy, maybe a copy of a letter Collins wrote and tucked into the file.

"How long has it been since anyone used carbon paper?" I asked Persuasion, who was ensconced in his usual spot at the French doors, staring at the bushes bordering my porch.

I put the letter back in the file and set the stack to one side. Perhaps these were the papers Mr. Collins had told his son about. Maybe Luke didn't know the old man already handed them off to me. I'd talk to him about it later. Right now, it was Sunday morning, my time to relax over the newspaper, drink a leisurely cup of coffee, then work on my Natural Girl article and my next novel without any interruptions or distractions.

I took my paper, coffee, and cat and went to the porch to lounge on my wicker couch. The *Barn and Bugle* didn't have a Sunday edition, so I had the *Des Moines Register* delivered, a much beefier paper than the local. I worked my way through the sports section, home and garden, regional news, and national news, and was just getting started on arts and entertainment when my phone rang.

My friends knew that Sundays were sacrosanct for me. I checked the number on the phone's LED, but I didn't recognize it. I considered letting it bounce to voice mail but remembered Luke Collins and reasoned it might be him. "Hello?"

"Miss Austin, this is Fitzgerald Williams. I was wondering if you have some time today to chat."

No, I wanted to say. It's Sunday. I don't want to deal with assholes today. Instead I asked, "What about, Dr. Williams?"

There was a brief hesitation. "I apologize. You're right. I should have used your title. You do have a PhD, after all."

"I don't care about protocol. Could we talk tomorrow perhaps? I have a busy day planned." A busy day planned for lounging in my faded shorts and raggedy T-shirt, editing and writing and generally enjoying myself without snobbish college professors.

"I feel we've gotten off on the wrong foot and I'd like to make amends. Perhaps I could take you to lunch? Or could we meet for coffee, later today?"

"Dr. Williams, it's irrelevant what foot we're on. I doubt we'll be socializing any time in the near future, so—"

"I'm asking you on a date."

I pulled the phone away from my ear and stared at it, not sure I'd heard correctly. "I beg your pardon?"

"I'm asking you out. I'd appreciate an opportunity to get to know you better." He cleared his throat. "I know that you may not be inclined to give me the time of day, but I'd like to talk to you and perhaps change your first impression of me."

"You're dating Ann Burge," I pointed out. "I may

not like Ann, in fact, I may detest her, but I don't poach on another woman's—"

"Ann and I are friends and nothing more. We are not dating."

He said it with such finality I had the feeling that this was a sore point with him. I sat up straighter in my chair. This was getting interesting. "Does Ann know that?"

"If you'd rather not go out with me, just say so." He was beginning to sound peeved.

"I'm just startled, that's all." I stalled, trying to gather my scattered thoughts. Ben said that Williams and Ann were dating, yet here was Williams saying that no, they weren't. Very interesting. "Perhaps we could meet later today," I suggested. "There's a small place in Longbarn near City Hall, across from Netherfield Park, called the Oxford Inn. It's a small hotel but it's also a bar and cafe. We could meet there if you'd like. They have coffee, wine, sandwiches. Happy hour starts at four."

He gave a shaky laugh. "Thank you. This was far more difficult than I thought it would be. It's been a long time since I've asked a woman on a date."

"Well, no offense, but from the way Ann hangs on to you, you don't appear to have had much difficulty at all."

"Looks can be deceiving. I'll see you there at four o'clock." He hung up before I could agree or disagree about the time.

I tried to recapture my Sunday mood, but it was difficult. In the back of my mind was a nagging little worry about my upcoming "date". I finished reading the newspaper then spent a few hours in my study, working on my novel in fits and starts. I had better luck with my Nature Girl article because that just needed polishing. At three o'clock, I emailed it to Joan Murray then went to my bedroom to change clothes.

After a few brief angst-filled moments of trying on and discarding outfits, I settled on lightweight blue slacks and my favorite knit top, patterned like a Paris street scene. I had never been to Paris, but it's as I imagined it would be with a rain-washed avenue and people sipping wine in outdoor cafes. I slipped on a pair of blue sandals, brushed my hair, dabbed on makeup, and was out the door without stopping to reconsider my appearance.

As I backed down the driveway and spied the Collins house in the distance, I remembered the bundle of papers from Mr. Collins. I considered going back for the papers to show them to Luke Collins, but it was close to four o'clock and I prided myself on my punctuality. I made a mental note to call him about the papers tomorrow.

Downtown Longbarn was quiet with only a few cars in front of the Oxford Inn and the Birmingham Diner. The town didn't really possess a sparkling nightlife, but there were a few smaller bars and cafes scattered here and there. I parked in the lot next to Netherfield Park, noting a stylish gray BMW parked at the far side of the space, away from any potential dings and dents.

I entered through the glass front door and went right toward the dining area, a smallish space big enough for five tall-backed wooden booths and a dozen white-clothed tables. Williams sat in a booth on the right, near the front window. The cocktail lounge was adjacent to the dining area and I glimpsed George Wick through the entryway, talking to several other men. I hurried to join Williams before George could spot me.

Williams stood when I neared him, smiling and revealing deep dimples at the sides of his mouth. He was simply dressed in light khakis and a contrasting brown shirt with the sleeves rolled up. The colors suited his dark hair shot through with gray and his golden tan, and the style emphasized his broad shoulders and narrow waist. He had a strong, square sort of face and his eyes, puppy brown behind the horn-rimmed glasses, were large and slightly tipped at the ends, making them appear very expressive.

"I'm pleased you came," he said. "I was afraid I'd made a fool of myself on the phone. I hope you don't mind, but I ordered a selection of appetizers. That seemed appropriate for cocktail hour." He gestured toward the dark marble table where two glasses of red wine sat next to a large tray of crudité, chicken wings, and other assorted fried munchies.

"That's fine with me." I slid into the booth opposite where he'd been sitting and after a brief hesitation, he resumed his seat. "It's not often an author gets a chance to talk to a reviewer, especially one with such a negative opinion." I held up a hand when he started to speak. "I don't object to your review, but I do object to the rather condescending tone in which it was written."

"Surely you can admit that the romance genre is often rather light on literary merit?" He peered at me over the tops of his glasses, his eyes intent on mine.

He didn't offer me one of the glasses of wine, so I ordered from the waitress then turned back to the conversation, marshalling arguments in my head. "I'll bet you that more romance novels are finished than so-called literary books. What do you have against popular culture? Twain wrote for a popular audience and now he's considered a classic."

He sipped his wine. "A classic is hardly a literary work."

I took a piece of celery from the hors d'oeuvres tray on the table and dabbed it in dip. "How do you define a literary work? One that students are forced to read in college? Something by Joyce, perhaps. Or maybe Henry James. I personally adore James but he's hard going for most people. I equate literary fiction as something dense and rather unintelligible."

Williams nodded. "That's a familiar argument. Some fiction does require a great deal of effort to be understood."

"And I suppose that means it's worthwhile?"

"Don't you think that something requiring effort is more satisfying than something that comes easily?"

I leaned back when the waitress set two glasses of white wine in front of me. "Ah. Happy hour. Thank you." I picked up one glass and took a hefty swallow. "I don't equate effort with enjoyment," I said, returning to the argument. "I'd rather write something that people want to read than write something just to please a few critics at the New York Times. My argument with you is that you judged the genre, not the work."

He leaned back in the booth. "But I can't separate the two, can I?"

"Of course, you can." I stabbed the celery into the dip again.

"I'm sorry. This hasn't gone the way I wanted." He

twirled the wine in his glass and appeared so contrite I relented.

"Does that mean you'll re-read my book with a new eye?"

He was so surprised I knew that thought never crossed his mind. "I doubt I'll have the time. I'm doing two reviews a month for the newspaper, and Miss Murray asked me to do several other reviews, rather informally. I'd like to do those in a timely manner for her. I think she's concerned about the quality of authorship at the newspaper."

"She did mention that she wanted you to review some of the columnists. It's always nice to get an outsider's view." He winced and I knew I'd struck a nerve. "Perhaps you can satisfy another curiosity of mine. Why did you move here? We're out of the way compared to some of the more prestigious Eastern schools."

He tilted his head and the dim light over the booth lit his glasses, obscuring his eyes. "I'm teaching because I enjoy teaching. It's hard to be a teacher and a scholar. Most colleges require that an instructor do both. You're fortunate to be teaching where such requirements aren't so stringent." He moved his head and I saw his inquisitive brown eyes.

I focused on filling my small plate with appetizers. "I have a good job at the Community College. I enjoy it."

"Wouldn't you rather be at Derby?" He leaned forward and also added a few items to his plate, probably concerned that I might empty it before he had a chance.

I wondered how much Ann had told him about the

old scandal that drove me away from Derby College. "Why would I? You just said how competitive it was and how you envied me because I didn't have to worry about that." I munched on delicious little corned-beef bites dipped in horseradish sauce. "You never answered my original question. Why leave a more prestigious Eastern school and come here?"

Williams sipped more wine, apparently thinking. "Have you ever had something happen to you that fundamentally changed how you view the world?"

I shot him a disbelieving look, but he just regarded me with alert curiosity. I considered saying, *Like being fired from a teaching job and having your reputation besmirched? Something like that?* but restrained myself. "I suppose I have."

His gaze went to Netherfield Park, across the street. "My father was a respected member of the community where I lived. He died four years ago, and I suddenly realized that I was following in his footsteps. Those weren't bad footsteps to follow in, but they weren't mine." His gaze swung back to me. "I had never truly taken a chance."

I smiled. "Iowa? You think Iowa is taking a chance? You make it sound like the Amazon or something."

Williams smiled, too, and his dimples made another appearance. They softened his face, giving him a mischievous appearance. "Well, to me it is. There is so much space here. So much land. I'm accustomed to urban areas with highways and towns and people." He turned slightly to view the outside again, at the gentle slope of the park. "Here there is so much beautiful emptiness. At first it was so very alien to me, so foreign. But now the thought of being in a large city makes me shudder. I'm sure if I had to adapt again, I could, but I would miss this."

His candor caught me by surprise. Most people didn't see the beauty in the landscape here. It was something subtle, not showy like mountains or the ocean. Iowa had a peaceful, verdant loveliness that was relaxing and intriguing at the same time. "I'm surprised you purchased land here. You must have known that land wouldn't be buildable. Did you buy it as an investment?"

"Partly. When I purchased it, the funding for the road hadn't been approved. Collins assured me that the funding debate had been going on for decades and no decision would be immediately forthcoming." Williams smiled wryly. "Then a few months later the project was given the green light by the planning commission."

"Mr. Collins? You bought the land from him?"

Williams nodded. "I think it was part of his inheritance. His father ceded the land to him when he turned thirty. He decided he had no use for it, so I purchased it directly from him."

I leaned back. "Wait a minute. You bought the land from Luke Collins?"

"Yes, Ann introduced us. She and he were childhood friends. She mentioned he had land to sell and I wanted land where I might possibly build, if my job becomes permanent. He has a large amount of land near the fen, which will be usable land if the road goes through. Also, some land further south where a new development will go in."

Odd. I thought Ann and Luke hadn't seen each other in years, or at least that was the impression I had the previous night. Then Williams' words soaked in. "Wait a minute. You're in a tenure track position, aren't you?"

An errant curl bobbed on his forehead when he shook his head. "The college is reassessing all tenured positions. Ann was upset by the change in policy." He shrugged. "It won't really affect me. I plan to retire in a few years anyway, but she had hopes of obtaining tenure. However, her—" He stopped. "Well, that's not for me to discuss. Suffice it to say, Ann cares deeply about her position at Derby and in the community."

I almost strangled on my wine. Williams was either naive or crazy. Or both. Ann cared about Ann and didn't give a shit about the community. But maybe I was prejudiced. Oh, hell. Of course, I was prejudiced.

"Well, isn't this cozy? Fitz Williams and pretty little Jane, having a bit of fun."

I glanced behind me. George Wick was swaggering out of the bar, heading across the dining area toward us. "Oh, Lord have mercy," I muttered. "Not him."

"I'm shocked, Jane," George drawled. "I thought we had an understanding? Quid pro quo? I scratch your back and you scratch mine?"

Williams' eyes narrowed. "Am I interrupting something?" he asked icily, his gaze going from me to George.

"What?" I leaned away from George when he swayed to a stop next to me.

"I saw you and him in the parking lot the other night." Williams pushed his plate away from him. "If I'm in the way, just let me know."

I glared at him. "What do you think you saw?"

"I know what I saw. You and him in an embrace."

71

George beamed at Williams, the glass of whiskey in his hand tilting dangerously near my arm. "Fitz, old friend. I haven't seen much of you since you moved to town. Seems like you're keeping busy." He leered down at me. "Did you know Fitz and I grew up together?"

"We didn't exactly grow up together," Williams snapped. "We went to the same college for a year or two. As I recall you got into difficulty with a young lady there and had to leave."

"And as I recall," George said with heavy sarcasm, "the young lady was your girlfriend. She got tired of being with you and chose to be with me." He waved a hand in dismissal, revealing sweat stains under the arm of his gold golf shirt. "I didn't like it there, anyway. I came back here and finished my law degree."

Williams regarded him with cool disdain. "Are you a lawyer or an attorney?"

"What's the difference?" I wanted to bite my tongue when Williams looked through me. Damn condescending asshole, I thought.

"An attorney is a lawyer, but a lawyer isn't always an attorney. Isn't that right, George?" Williams' gaze swept over George, taking in his rumpled shirt and dark blue pants. "An attorney can operate in a court, but a lawyer can only provide legal advice unless that lawyer has passed the bar exam in his or her state."

George stiffened and when he tried to straighten, he had to grab the booth's finial for support. Bourbon splashed on the booth, the floor, and on my arm. I muttered a curse and started to dab it off my blouse. "It's a minor distinction. Simply a matter of taking a test or two. As you well know, since you're busy poaching clients and dispensing legal advice."

"What's that mean?" I asked.

Williams regarded us both with cool disdain. "I was asked by one of George's clients to provide an independent legal opinion on a private matter. I did so, and it may have reflected poorly on George." He regarded George. "Am I right?"

"You're a lawyer?" I asked. My experience with lawyers was mostly negative, leaving me with the firm belief that most of them were arrogant assholes who didn't deserve half the money they got for their services. That explained a lot about Williams.

Then I remembered the note from Mr. Collins. *I am seeking legal advice*, he said. Did he contact Fitz Williams and ask for help?

George flushed a deep red. "Since you haven't taken the bar exam in Iowa, that's all you can do. Dispense advice."

"Not quite." Williams swished the wine in his glass. "It's a tedious legal distinction, but there is reciprocity with other states. I can act as an attorney here in a limited capacity. But I don't plan to, if that's what concerns you."

George's eyes narrowed as he struggled to process that statement. Then he gave up because he turned his attention to me, smiling broadly. "I'm sure Jane doesn't care about any of that that. She and I are old friends."

Williams twirled the wine in his glass thoughtfully. "Indeed."

I snatched my purse and bolted out of the booth so fast I could have knocked George over. "Looks can be deceiving."

"Oh, that is so true," George's bleary gaze went

from me to Williams then back to me. "Take Jane, here. She seems so sweet and innocent. If you're not careful, I'll tell the police about how you influenced that old man. Old Mr. Collins didn't stand a chance against her," he said to Williams. "You know her history, right? She has a habit of bewitching vulnerable men."

Williams stared at me, his jaw tight. "You're a matched pair."

George apparently didn't hear him, because he nodded, his head bobbing like a ragdoll's. "She's a regular harlot."

I longed to hit Williams, but George was closer. "You son of a bitch." I slapped him as hard as I could.

Chapter 5

George staggered back from the force of my blow, sidestepping the table behind him and coming to rest against the doorframe leading to the bar. The bartender, alerted to trouble, hurried into the room and, taking George by the arm, righted him.

"Thanks for the drink," I said to Williams. "I'll leave now, though, before anybody sees you in my company. God forbid I should tarnish your reputation."

"Apparently you aren't as worried about your own reputation." Williams pulled out a wallet and extracted some bills, leaving the money on the table. "I'll make sure George gets home safely. Good night, Miss Austin." He brushed by me, his face set and hard.

I was so angry I was shaking. I considered going after him but instead I sank back down in the booth and downed my glass of wine, conscious of the furtive glances from the six tables where diners sat. I peeked through the window and saw Williams holding George by the left arm and steering him across the street, another man holding George's right arm. They walked to the far end of the parking lot where Williams' stylish sedan sat.

"Sorry for that," the waitress said, appearing at my side. "He's an asshole when he drinks. Of course, he drinks all the time so he's always an asshole, I guess."

"No, I'm sorry. I shouldn't have hit him."

"He deserved it. No problem. Take your time." She waved to the appetizers sitting on the table and my other glass of wine. "It's paid for."

Damn it, she was right. I rested back in the booth, determined to enjoy myself at Dr. Williams' expense. His behavior was galling especially given the somewhat flirtatious way he acted earlier. I smeared another cracker with smoked salmon and mulled over what just happened. I was halfway through my second glass of wine when it struck me.

Williams undoubtedly heard the old story about me seducing a student at Derby College when I taught there. I'm sure Ann told him, damn her soul. I left Derby even though nothing was proved against me and the student later recanted. Then Williams saw me with George in the parking lot, in a supposedly hot embrace. And then George made that crack about old Mr. Collins. And Williams saw me last night in the study talking to Luke Collins. And what was it George said? He made some snide remark about a girl in college, a girl Williams was dating. There was probably bad blood between the two of them.

I shook my head. It didn't matter now. Williams had somehow added it up to mean that I was, in George's words, a harlot. Lord knows why he asked me out. Maybe he was giving me the benefit of the doubt and George just screwed it up. Or maybe—

"Oh, shit, what does it matter?" I finished my wine and left the cafe. It shouldn't matter, but for some reason I did care what Dr. D. Fitzgerald Williams thought, damn it. He thought I was a cheap tramp and I could do nothing to change his mind.

I drove home, unaccountably depressed. I tried to

work on my novel but my mind kept straying, replaying the awful look on Williams' face when he accused me of consorting with George. I finally gave up and drifted into the living room. A few minutes with the remote control convinced me I'd be better off with a movie. I was thumbing through my DVD collection when the phone rang. I picked it up, discs tumbling to the floor. "Hello?"

"I want to apologize. I jumped to conclusions. George told me that he tried to force himself on you and you resisted. He made it very clear what happened, in the crudest sort of language. I should have known. It's the sort of thing George does, preying on defenseless women." Williams sounded contrite and also angry. I couldn't tell if he was angry because of me or because of what happened to me, but either way, it was irrelevant.

"George is an asshole and I'm not defenseless. Apology not accepted." I hung up.

The phone rang again, and I turned off the ringer. I poured myself a glass of wine, popped in *Mama Mia*, and settled down for a fun-filled evening of singing and laughter.

****

The next morning, I stopped at the newspaper office on my way to school to verify that Joan received my Nature Girl article which I emailed the evening before.

"I got it," she confirmed when I spied her at the front counter that separated the offices from the public. "And I did ask Dr. Williams to do a review of our feature writers, so when I get his evaluation of Nature Girl, I'll be sure to share it with you."

"Don't bother. I'm sure it will be as big a disappointment to him as my novel was." I looked beyond her to the open space that housed four desks, three of which were occupied. "A busy news day?"

"Monday. Weekend wrap-up. Since we don't do a paper on Saturday or Sunday there's always a lot of summarizing to do. Did you hear that the funeral for Mr. Collins is postponed? There's an autopsy being done and apparently that takes time."

"Good heavens. I thought the poor man had a heart attack or something."

"I guess whenever there's an unusual death, they have to investigate."

"Unusual?"

Joan grinned. "Read about it tonight in the newspaper."

I smiled wryly. "Good marketing. Talk to you later."

"Oh, by the way." She walked around the counter to join me at the front door. "I heard about an altercation at the Oxford last night. It spilled into the parking lot across the street, where George Wick was decked by someone. The bartender had to call him a cab to get him home."

"Really?" I doubted Williams decked George. I'll bet what happened was that George was drunk, he took a swing and fell down. "Is anybody going to press charges?"

Joan shrugged. "Dunno. I was driving through town last night and saw your Mini Cooper in the parking lot. You didn't see anything did you? I always like to get corroborating information if I can."

"Not a clue." I was thankful the morning sun

streamed through the open door and forced me to put on my sunglasses. "I didn't see a thing. If you find out, let me know."

She laughed. "Or else you'll read it in the paper."

I left the office and drove east to the Community College campus on the edge of town. Bright June sunlight heated the damp air, and by the time I got to the air-conditioned building where my office was located I was hot and bothered, hot because of the temperatures and bothered to think that Williams and George Wick got into a tussle over me.

I called Ben as soon as I reached my little cubbyhole of an office. I got his answering machine and I left a message, asking him to call me as soon as he could. If George was in trouble, his wife Lydia would turn to Ben for help, or so I reasoned.

I went downstairs and outside briefly to get to my class building, where my students' attitudes seemed to reflect the heat. My classes were sluggish and apathetic, with one student in Social Literature class whining that, "I'm majoring in Landscape Design. What do I need to know about *Moby Dick* for?"

I fixed the girl with a stern eye. "You may have an opportunity to chat with wealthy clients, and believe me when I say that most of them know *Moby Dick*. It behooves you to be able to talk to them without embarrassment."

She subsided with a pout and I knew many others in the class felt the same way. I plowed ahead with a summary of Hawthorne and Melville and breathed a sigh of relief when the class was finished.

I emerged from the classroom and walked right into Ben Raines, who waited for me outside the doorway. "I called you this morning," I said by way of greeting. "I left a message."

"I know. That's why I'm here. Do you know what happened?" He walked to the side of the wide hallway, away from the bustle of students around the door.

"About what?" I asked as I followed him.

"Williams came to my office this morning and demanded to know why you left Derby College."

"Demanded? That's a bit high-handed of him, isn't it?" I tried to sound cool about it but inwardly I was gleeful. Ben's next words dampened my happiness.

"He talked to Ann about it and of course she gave him a skewed version of it all. I pointed out that she was involved in what occurred and couldn't be trusted." Ben's sad brown eyes reflected his disappointment in Ann Burge.

"What did you tell him?" I asked, leading the way to the exit to go to my office.

"That a student accused you of inappropriate behavior, but he later recanted." Ben pushed open the door for me. "And I told him the faculty at Derby did not support you and were generally ass-hats."

I laughed at his wording, which was so like Ben. "Thank you for your support. You and a handful of other people were the only ones who believed me."

He grinned. "Anyone who knows you knows you have much better taste in men. Anyway, that's only one reason I came to see you."

We emerged into the moist afternoon heat. Ben made a turn toward my office building, but I gestured to the parking lot. "I'm done for the day. Come over to the house? It's too hot to stand around and chat."

"Just for a minute. I have to get back for a faculty

meeting." Ben and I skirted a group of co-eds in scanty shorts and tops who lounged on towels on the grassy lawn, oblivious or uncaring about skin cancer, sunburn, or humidity. "Luke Collins called me. He said he was giving you some papers that his father left to SOFT."

I nodded. "He mentioned it at the party on Saturday."

"I think those papers are important. George mentioned to Lydia that there's a question of land ownership for the fen. Until it's settled, the state can't proceed with the road project."

"What? How would George know about that?"

"George's father was old Mr. Collins' lawyer, back in the day, I guess. George was going through some of his father's files and found information about it. He mentioned it to Lydia, and she told me when she stopped by my office today." Ben looked away from me when he spoke, which told me he had given in and funded Lydia's latest pleas for money. "I thought you should know about it because Luke will be handing over some old papers and there might be something in there that's useful. For our cause, I mean."

Our cause. I felt a pang of guilt. Ben sincerely cared about the ecological impact of the road construction. My concerns were more mundane and selfish. I worried first about the impact on my life in the neighborhood and secondly about the turtles and other fauna. "You didn't have to drive over here just to tell me. But thanks for doing it."

"I was hoping maybe Luke handed off the papers to you already and I could examine them."

"He said he would drop them at the house. I told him to leave them on the porch if I wasn't home. We can go check, I guess."

"Could we? If we can find something in those papers that helps us, maybe we can stop this project before it gets too much momentum."

"What time is your meeting?"

"Three."

"Okay, just meet me at my place. We'll see if Luke left anything and if he didn't, you can always go to the Collins house and see if he's there."

Ben smiled. "Perfect. I should have plenty of time to do that and get back to campus. Thanks, Jane. This means a lot to me. If we can save that wildlife refuge it means we can finally strike a blow for common sense over greed. I told Dr. Williams that, but I don't think he really understands what's at stake."

"Oh, I think he does. He strikes me as being a smart cookie." We paused at an intersection in the sidewalk and I headed to the right toward the faculty lot.

"Not too smart of him to tangle with George Wick. Lydia was furious with George and him for fighting."

I stopped in my tracks. "What?"

"Didn't you hear? I thought it was all over town. George and he got into a fight last night. I'm not sure what it was about, but Williams has a bruised hand and Lydia said George has a black eye." Ben grinned. "Too bad Williams didn't flatten him. I'll go get my car and meet you at your place." He hurried off before I could question him further.

I walked more slowly down the tree-shaded sidewalk to the parking lot. Was Williams truly having a change of heart? The fact that he went to Ben and asked about what happened ten years ago, and the fact that he and George got into a fight—didn't that add up to—

Add up to what? Granted, Williams had asked me out, but maybe he was a spy, trying to discover details about our committee's work. Although admittedly, we talked very little about the road project. I unlocked my car and slid into the oven-hot interior. Dr. Williams, his opinions, and his behavior were really no concern of mine. He came from one world, old money and the East. I was Midwest and making ends meet. "Never the twain shall meet," I muttered.

Ben's drive was slightly shorter than mine since he parked in the visitor parking lot, so he got to my house first and was leaving his car when I arrived. I parked in the garage and walked outside to meet him on my porch.

"Nothing here," he said, checking the porch furniture outside my study.

"Let me check the mailbox." I went across the street and retrieved the day's mail, sorting through the letters quickly. "Nothing here," I told Ben. "Come inside. You can call Luke Collins and see if he's home."

Ben began to follow me into the house but we both stopped when Ann Burge's snazzy little red sports car pulled into my drive. Ann hopped out and strode toward us, cool and stylish in her pale yellow sundress. "I'm glad I caught you at home," she said to me, handing me a manila envelope. "Luke asked me to drop this off this morning on my way to work and I forgot. Then when Fitz asked me to deliver his thank-you note, I remembered." She smiled and held out a small envelope. "He's very old-fashioned that way. He wanted to thank you for the party, even though he came as my guest."

"When did Luke give it to you?" I asked, setting down my book bag to open the bulky envelope.

"What do you mean?"

Her sharp tone of voice made me look up in surprise. "Nothing. He and I chatted about it on Saturday, and I thought he would drop it off on Sunday."

Ann shrugged, one tanned shoulder lifting negligently. "Luke and I had lunch together yesterday and he mentioned how busy he was. I volunteered to drop it off when I drove past on my way to school, but I forgot. He said that his father wanted your group to have some old papers. You know, it's odd, but my mother seems to be taking Mr. Collins' death hard."

"Well, they were contemporaries," I said. "She's known him for a long time."

"I suppose so. Or maybe I'm imagining it, and it just appears she's getting frailer and less, oh, I don't know, less robust." Ann gave a brief, insincere smile. "She is an elderly woman, after all. I guess I shouldn't be surprised if she starts to fail."

Fail? Old Mrs. Burge? I always thought that she was so ornery she'd tell Death to leave her alone if he ever came knocking on her door.

"Maybe now that he's gone, she's just wondering about the lawsuit," Ben suggested.

Ann's attention zeroed in on him. "What do you know about the lawsuit?"

"The never-ending court case, isn't it?" Ben smiled apologetically when Ann's eyes narrowed in anger. "From what I've heard, it's been going on for years."

"Well, you heard wrong. It was settled decades ago. Mr. Collins was just being obstinate about a few minor points in the contract for deed, that's all."

Luke Collins had said the same thing but slightly different. According to him, it was Mrs. Burge who was being obstinate and causing the delays. I suppose that was his point of view. "Does Luke inherit the lawsuit?" I asked.

"I suppose he must," Ben said. "Just like George inherited it."

"George?" I handed the envelope to Ben.

"George's father was the attorney of record. When his father died, he inherited a lot of the old man's clients." Ben peeked inside the envelope. "You were away from town when that happened. George went East to law school and came back and went into practice with his father before his father died."

"I told you," Ann said with exaggerated patience. "There isn't anything to inherit. Besides, you can't believe a word George Wick says. Honestly, everybody knows that."

"You're the historian in our group, Ben. Let me know if there's anything there for me to review." I remembered the other envelope full of old papers. "Hold on a second. Mr. Collins dropped off some papers the other day and they're sitting on my desk. You may as well go through those, too. It won't take me a minute to find them. You've got time before your meeting, right? It doesn't start until three?"

"What do you mean?" Ann asked, her voice once again sharp.

I ducked into my study, just inside the entryway. I left the mail and my book bag in my office and swept up the accordion folder still sitting there. I emerged through the porch doors and handed Ben the bulky folder. "I found that in my mailbox the other day with a note from Mr. Collins. You may as well go through it at the same time as you go through the other ones."

"What is it?" Ann asked, sidling nearer Ben to get a peek at the accordion folder.

"Are you sure? He left it to you." Ben tucked the manila envelope under his arm while he peeked inside the folder.

"He left it to our group. I was just convenient. Thanks for dropping it off, Ann. Do know when Mr. Collins' funeral will be?"

"Why would I know?" She stepped back when Ben closed the folder.

"You're in touch with Luke, so I thought he might have mentioned it. I'm sure our group will want to send flowers." I looked at Ben for confirmation and he nodded.

"I'm not sure. There will be something in the paper." She walked away, her skirt swirling around her legs, the picture of indifference.

"I'll catalog these papers and let you know if anything interesting pops out," Ben said.

"I doubt there is. After all, if Mr. Collins had the opportunity to stop the construction project, why didn't he do it a long time ago?"

"I suppose," Ben conceded. "But it might be interesting, nonetheless. Maybe Charlotte and I can examine them tonight."

"Oh, really? You and the delightful Dr. Bing are having a date?"

Ben appeared so pleased with himself I was hard-pressed not to laugh aloud. "She's coming to my house for dinner. She and Dr. Williams really are just friends. He's confided in Charlotte that he's intrigued by a lady here in town, and she told me she was encouraging him to pursue his interests."

"I'm sure Ann will be pleased to hear that." I glanced at my watch. "You'd better get on the road if you're going to that faculty meeting."

"Not Ann," Ben said with a smug smile. "You."

"Bullshit," I enunciated. "Trust me. The delightful Dr. Williams has no interest in a fallen woman like me. God forbid I should besmirch his reputation."

"That's not what Charlotte told me. She said that she talked to him last night and he was worried that he'd done something to upset you and he was sure you'd never speak to him again."

"He did, and I won't." I went to the study doors. "Good-bye, Ben. Talk to you later." I went inside and firmly closed the French doors behind me.

I wasn't sure whether to be angry or bemused by this latest turn of events. On the one hand, Williams was blabbing to all and sundry that he upset me. I hated to have my business bandied about like that. On the other hand, it was marvelous to think he might be stewing about it.

"Or, as my mother used to say, on the other hand, he had five fingers," I said to Persuasion, who ambled in to remind me it was time for food. "It may not mean a thing. There's no use thinking about it now." I took my mail and followed my long-haired feline to the kitchen where I fed him and poured myself a glass of lemonade.

I went to the back porch, kicked off my shoes, and

relaxed on my chaise lounge. I had essays to grade and coursework to prepare, but that could wait for an hour or two. Summer school was sometimes a chore to teach because the classes were accelerated to fit into a tighter schedule. But it also meant a welcome paycheck in June and July with the month of August off. I was finally recovering financially from the loss of my job at Derby, thanks in part to a small inheritance when my mother died which allowed me to pay off my house.

I skimmed through the newspaper. Despite Joan's teasing innuendo, I spied only a brief note about Collins' death. *Police continue investigation* with a couple of paragraphs about the fen. The article noted that Collins was found by a hiker who was walking through the nature preserve and spied the body.

I sorted the rest of my mail, finally coming to the letter Ann delivered from Williams. Despite what she said, I was certain it was not a thank-you note for my party, and my suspicions were confirmed when I tore it open and read.

I have no idea how to apologize for my boorish behavior on Sunday evening. My only defense is that I am familiar with George Wick and his effect on women. I've known two women who have fallen under his spell. One was my younger sister. I won't go into the nasty details, but she was a young girl at the time, only in high school. I was able to intervene before any lasting damage was done.

The other was a young woman I knew in college. Despite what George said, she and I were not romantically involved but we were good friends. George seduced her then left her when he discovered she was hoping for a more permanent relationship. She wasn't the rich girl he thought she was. He returned home to Iowa, and my friend was left with an unwanted pregnancy and a broken heart.

When I saw you and George together, I assumed the worst—the worst of George, not you, and I hope you'll believe me when I say that. George and I have an acrimonious history, and what I've learned about him since I moved here has only increased my dislike of him. George made a very crude reference to the supposed scandal concerning your departure from Derby College, and suddenly some of his words made sense—or so I thought.

I asked Ann about what happened, and I also asked several colleagues. Their accounts convinced me I needed to find another source of truth. I discussed it with Ben Jaines, who told me what I believe to be a true account of the events that forced you from your teaching job—the job that I now hold.

I won't apologize for stepping into the position you were forced to vacate, but I do offer another apology for my academic assumptions. I thought you had little knowledge of the era in which you set your novel and I was predisposed to read the book with a critical eye. When I reviewed your book, I made an error—that you were a romance novelist and thus not a real author. I can't fault anything in your book regarding the historical period and the social conventions of that time. I apologize for implying that I did, but I warn you. I still feel your heroine was disingenuous and your hero was too trusting.

Perhaps you will give me the opportunity to argue those points with you at some time in the future. I think I have apologized enough in this letter, but if I haven't,

I'm willing to offer more apologies in person.
  Fitz Williams

I folded the letter and stared thoughtfully at my garden. Good heavens, if what he said was true, George really was a bastard of the worst kind. I had a sneaking suspicion that Williams wasn't exaggerating anything. I could well imagine George preying on some helpless young girl—or girls.

I went into the kitchen and put together a salad for my supper. Were my assumptions about Williams wrong? Yes, he was over-confident and a bit arrogant, but the letter did sound sincere. That question nagged me through my meal and my evening of grading papers and other schoolwork. It wasn't until I sat down to work on my novel that a revelation struck me.

I was as guilty as Williams of making assumptions. I presumed that he was some uppity Eastern snob, slumming with us Midwesterners. I had formed an opinion about him based on his review of my book, his association with Ann Burge, and a few comments made by other people. I was not evaluating him on his own merits, as it were.

My phone rang, and I checked the caller ID. "Ben, I thought you were entertaining tonight?" I asked. "What are you doing calling me?"

"Charlotte and I were going through those papers. She has a much better understanding of property documents than I do." He sounded gleeful, as if a date poring over moldering documents was a night out on the town. "We found something that I think will be very useful. Charlotte will do some more research about it, but I think it might solve our problems."

"Really?" I stared through my French doors at the

darkness beyond my porch. "What kind of information did you find?"

"Some papers regarding transfer of land ownership. Fascinating things. Really, compared to English history, America is so young. These papers only go back sixty or seventy years. Compare that to ownership papers in England, where property ownership can stretch back several generations."

"He's exaggerating." I heard Charlotte Bing in the background, her voice full of laughter. "But not by much."

"It sounds like you're having a marvelous time."

"We are. This has been fun. Thanks for letting me examine them."

"Thank you for letting *us* examine them," Charlotte called out.

I envied Ben his convivial companionship. "Do you want to get together tomorrow and go over what you found?" I asked.

"Sure. I'm teaching class in the morning. How about the afternoon? I'll come over to your house."

"I want to come, too," Charlotte said. "It's my find, too."

I brought up my calendar on the computer. "Georgie and I are reviewing gardens for this year's Garden Walk tomorrow," I said. "Why don't you two come over for dinner tomorrow night? We can throw a burger on the grill."

"Hold on, I'll check." I heard muffled voices then Ben said, "Sounds good. We'll be there around five or so. See you then."

"I'll have the wine chilled," I promised before hanging up the phone. I added an entry to my online calendar then went to the kitchen to put some frozen hamburger in the fridge to defrost. When I walked back through the living room to my study, I glanced at the back porch and I thought I glimpsed movement in the yard.

I went to the porch doors and flicked on the switch for the outside lights. A glimmer of something light-colored showed at the edge of my yard, where the surrounding trees formed an impenetrable barrier between me and the nearest homes. Then it was gone, disappearing into the shrubby undergrowth.

I checked the door and made sure it was locked then went back to the study. My neighbor to the east had a golden lab who loved to roam the neighborhood, and it was probably just Tank out for his evening ramble. I continued working on my novel until my brain cells refused to cooperate any more, finally sleeping around eleven.

It was after midnight that my phone rang. I didn't recognize the number on my caller ID, but any time someone calls that late at night, I feel I need to answer. "Austin residence," I mumbled sleepily into the receiver.

"Jane? It's Charlotte Bing. I'm at the hospital. Can you come? It' Ben."

I sat up in bed, dislodging Persuasion from his spot near my ankles. "What? What happened?"

"The police called me. His house was broken into and he was hurt. Somebody attacked him."

Chapter 6

I rushed into the emergency room at the Derby County Hospital. Straight ahead was an oval waist-high wooden counter and on either side were alcoves with chairs. Behind the counter was a wall with two doors where I assumed the real emergency work was done. I started for the counter, but I spied Charlotte Bing sitting in an alcove that held six gray chairs and a table full of magazines. I detoured to her, slipping into the chair next to her. "What happened?"

"I found him," she said, dabbing her red-rimmed eyes with a hankie. "Thank God I did. My house keys and my car keys are on one of those connecting keychains and somehow my house keys got disconnected. Anyway, I got home, and I found I didn't have my house key. I just moved into this house a month or two ago and I hadn't gotten around to hiding a spare key outside. Long story short, I searched my car and the ground around the car but couldn't find my key. I decided I must have dropped it at Ben's house so I drove back there."

Well, that explained her clothing, a pretty red-striped top with dark slacks. Those were dating clothes, not middle-of-the-night emergency room clothes. She looked like she was ready for an evening of dancing except for her blotchy complexion and desperate expression. "How did you find him?"

"I rang the bell, but he didn't answer. His lights were still on, so I knocked. The door was open, I went in, and I found him." Her pale blue eyes were so wide she was like the proverbial deer in the headlights.

"And?" I prompted. A buzzing sound from the counter made me jerk. It was low and insistent, like an alarm clock in another room. "What's that?"

"I think they're paging somebody. It goes off now and then." Charlotte dabbed her nose. "I got into Ben's house and it was a mess. Furniture was turned over and books were pulled from the bookcase. His TV was on the floor. I couldn't believe it. I was there just an hour or so earlier and everything was fine. Now it was crazy, like a tornado went through the room."

"Where was Ben?"

"He was in his office. You know, down that little hallway on the right. He was lying on the floor. He was facedown, and when I knelt next to him I got blood on my knees and—" She was babbling, her face panicked.

I took her hand. "Charlotte, it's okay. Ben's here now and they're taking care of him. Was he shot? Could you tell what happened to him?"

"He was unconscious. The ambulance worker said it might be a stab wound. Who would do such a thing? Ben lived just a few blocks from campus. Manortown doesn't have crime like this. The worst that ever happens is an occasional drunk or a student who gets rowdy. I can't believe somebody broke into his house and robbed him and tried to kill him."

"Robbed him? Are you sure?"

Her head bobbed, blonde curls dancing. "He and I were going through those papers you gave him. They were in his office when I left. I think they were taken."

"What? Why would somebody take those?"

"Miss Bing?"

Charlotte and I both stood when a doctor in blue scrubs came into the alcove. "I'm Charlotte Bing. This is my friend and Ben's, Dr. Austin. How's Ben? Will he be okay?"

The doctor nodded. He was too young to be so tired. "He should make a full recovery. He was lucky. An inch or two more to the front and it would have nicked his heart or lungs. As it is, he has two broken ribs, he's lost some blood, and he has a concussion. We'll keep him under observation for at least a day. The police are talking to him now, then he'll be taken to a room. You can go with him if you want." He turned to go but paused. "Are you Jane, by any chance?"

I nodded.

One corner of the doctor's mouth quirked up in a smile. "Jane Austin. Quite a name. He was asking for you. He wants to talk to you."

"Probably about the papers that were stolen." I linked arms with Charlotte. "Let's make sure he's okay then you need to go home and get some rest. You've had a hell of a night."

Charlotte and I followed the doctor through a door behind the counter. As I suspected, this was where the medical work was done. Small curtained cubicles lined the walls, four on each side.

"I doubt I could sleep," Charlotte whispered. "I'll see boogie men invading my home."

"I don't think you have to worry about that." I lowered my voice when the doctor slowed near one of the curtained cubicles. "Whoever broke into Ben's house was after something specific. I don't think this was random."

The curtain was pulled back. A bandage covered one side of Ben's head but otherwise he didn't look too bad except he was deathly pale. Of course, most of him was tucked into hospital sheets or covered by a hospital gown, so I couldn't see his torso. Ben's eyes went to me then Charlotte then back to the uniformed policeman next to the bed, who was writing in a small spiral notebook.

"I'm Officer Carter, with the Manortown PD." The officer handed us each a business card, which I glanced at before stuffing it in my purse. "If any of you think of anything, please contact us." He turned his attention back to Ben. "Is this your friend?"

Ben nodded. "Jane, can you and Charlotte go to the house?" he whispered. "The police want to know if anything was taken. Anything of value, that is. Can you check my laptop? Any other small electronics?"

"Of course. I'll make sure Charlotte gets home okay then I'll check."

"I'll go with you," Charlotte volunteered. "You shouldn't be there alone." Officer Carter frowned at her. "I mean, maybe you'd like some company."

I hadn't even considered that, but she was right. "Okay, we'll check together."

Everybody cleared out of the way when two hospital staffers bustled into the cubicle. Ben was disconnected from gadgets there and was wheeled away, bed and all, to an elevator and from there to a room on the second floor. The police officer rode with him, asking questions the entire time, which gave me a good chance to hear what happened.

Apparently when Charlotte left his home, Ben

puttered around in the kitchen for a few minutes then began to turn off lights. The doorbell rang, and he went to answer it. When he unbolted the lock on the door, it was shoved open. Ben was hit on the head with something that made him black out momentarily. When he got his senses back, he was sprawled against the entryway wall, and a figure in dark clothes and a ski mask was trashing his living room.

Ben went after the person and that's when the intruder drew a knife. They fought. The person knifed him and ran down the hall. Ben staggered after and collapsed in the study. The last thing he saw was his attacker leaning over the table in the study where Ben had left the papers from old Mr. Collins.

Charlotte and I saw Ben settled in his room, and she assured him she'd contact the school to make sure his classes were canceled for the week. She and I left shortly after the policeman, who promised to meet us at Ben's house. "It has to be those papers," I told Charlotte while we walked in the hospital parking lot together.

"We won't know for sure until we go to his house and see what was taken. Ben might have passed out in the study, and maybe somebody went back through the house and took his television or something else." She sounded doubtful.

"He didn't have anything of value," I said, pausing by my car. "He had a computer, so I suppose that's worth something, and I think he had an iPad. I think he had some rare books, too. We'll have to see what was taken. I'll follow you, and you follow the cop, okay?"

Charlotte nodded and hurried to her car, a small sedan parked near the entrance. We followed the squad car, forming a somber parade through the dark town, past the college campus to Ben's two-story Cape Cod house.

Charlotte and I met Officer Carter at the front door. "Try not to touch anything if you can," he said, pulling latex gloves from one pocket and handing us each a pair. "If you do need to touch anything, make sure you have your gloves on."

"You'll fingerprint everything?" I asked, holding up the gloves in the porch light to see them better.

"It depends on what you find." He already had his gloves on, obviously more adept in their use than I was.

"Here, do this," Charlotte said. She blew into one glove and it puffed up like an udder. She slipped it on her hand before it was fully deflated.

"Good trick." I got my gloves on and we followed the officer into the house.

"I have to wear gloves a lot if I'm handling historical documents," she said. "A colleague at the London Museum showed me that trick."

"If you could focus on the living room and study, that would be helpful," Carter said. "I'll do a sweep through the other rooms and see if anything appears disturbed." He disappeared down the hall toward the kitchen at the back of the house before Charlotte or I could agree or disagree.

I went through the archway on the left and we entered the living room. "Good grief," I murmured, when I saw the mess there. One lamp burned brightly, the shade dangling crazily from the reflector bowl housing the bulb. I stepped carefully over piles of books, a shattered lamp, companion to the one illuminating the room, a tipped-up end table and chair, and other remnants of what used to be a cozy sitting area.

"They didn't take the TV," Charlotte said, pointing to the upended set in the corner. "Check over there. Ben's laptop was on the side table earlier in the evening."

I high-stepped over a pile of books and leaned on an upended chair to examine a corner. "It's gone. I can see the power cord, but the laptop is gone."

"He and I sorted through those papers, and Ben scanned most of them. He has a handheld portable scanner. That's the best way to handle historical documents. We sorted them here, and he scanned them then we moved into the study to spread them around."

"He made copies?" I straightened.

Charlotte nodded. "He planned to check with the Historical Society and see if they wanted to have some of the originals. He thought a few might be valuable. But the scanned copies were stored on his laptop and it's gone. What is in those papers that would merit someone trying to kill him?" Charlotte's shoulders sagged. "Jane, I thought he was dead. My God, when I saw him, I thought he was dead." Tears rolled down her cheeks. "I've wasted all this time not letting him know how I feel. Fitz told me I was silly for not telling Ben, but I was afraid Ben didn't feel the same way."

"Fitz? Dr. Williams?"

Charlotte nodded miserably. "Fitz and I have been friends for years, just like you and Ben are friends. When I told him that I was interested in Ben, Fitz told me I was crazy."

"Why on earth would he say that?" I turned in a slow circle, trying to see if anything else was missing.

"You have to know Fitz, I guess. He has sort of a cynical view of romance."

"No kidding," I murmured.

"He fell in love with a girl then he discovered she was only in it for his money. His family is really well off and they're big-wigs out East. Kind of like a low-key version of the Kennedys."

"Really? I had no idea. He doesn't seem like the big-wig type."

"That's just it. He isn't. He was miserable, trying to fit in just because it was expected of him. When I took the job here, he thought I was crazy. But I've been happy here, Jane. I love it. I talked Fitz into coming here. He looked down on Ben at first, and the college. But just recently he confessed he likes it here and he hopes to stay here." Charlotte picked her way through the mess to join me in the doorway. "He even told me that he likes Ben. Why, oh why, didn't I tell Ben how I felt?"

I put an arm around her, or rather, I tried to. Charlotte was taller than me and big-boned. "You can tell him now," I said. "I know he feels the same about you. He's just so damn shy. Come on, let's go check the study."

"Are you sure?" She followed me docilely, her pale blue eyes enormous. "Do you really think he feels that way?"

"I'm certain." I stopped on the threshold of Ben's study. His floor-to-ceiling bookcases were oddly untouched, the books lined up with a few awards and photographs interspersed with the volumes. Some of the books were very rare, and those were in a still intact locked glass case. To the left of the door was a large oak table where a map sat near an overturned lamp. Ben's desk, an old oak partner's desk with six drawers on either side of the kneehole, was littered with files, papers, and books.

I started into the room, but Charlotte grabbed my arm and pulled me to a stop. "He was right there," she whispered, pointing at the wood floor where a dark red stain intersected with the edge of a gold-and-red patterned area rug. "That's where I found him."

I skirted that spot and went to the desk. Charlotte went to the table. "We spread out most of the papers here. Ben wanted to check some of the information in the deeds to an old map he had." Charlotte shuffled through the papers on the tabletop. "That map is gone. So are the papers."

"The accordion file is here," I said, holding up the empty folder.

"What about his notebook?" Charlotte joined me at the desk, stepping over the stain on the floor. "He was jotting notes in a red spiral notebook."

"That's his turtle notebook. The one he used for SOFT and our campaign." I walked around the desk and rifled through the drawers. "Nothing here. Somebody took his SOFT notebook. Damn it, he had a bunch of useful information in that notebook."

Charlotte picked up a picture of Ben and his sisters from the desk. "I should call his sister, Lydia. She lives in Longbarn, doesn't she? Maybe she'd want to go to the hospital to be with him. I think his other sisters live out of state."

I sifted through the disorderly stack of papers on Ben's desk. "Lydia isn't exactly the nurturing type. Ben will call her himself tomorrow." Speaking of Lydia reminded me of George Wick. "Fitz Williams mentioned that he knew George Wick from college back East. Did you know him?"

Charlotte shook her head. "Fitz went to a different college than I did. I heard about him, though. Fitz had a friend who got into trouble and had to have an abortion because of George Wick. Fitz wasn't sure he wanted to move here when he knew where the college was located. He didn't want to run into Wick. But I convinced him the college is far enough away from Longbarn that he wouldn't run into Wick, so he decided to give Derby College a try. I think he's glad he did."

"He does seem happy at Derby," I said absently, shuffling through papers.

"When did you two talk about it?" Charlotte stared at me, her head tilted to one side, the picture of confused curiosity.

"He and I chatted the other day. He said he wished he could be someplace where he didn't have to worry about the whole publish or perish thing, but other than that he likes it here. But then he said it really didn't matter because he'd be retiring soon anyway."

"Interesting. I didn't realize you knew him so well."

I shrugged. "It's just something he mentioned. You know, in passing." I turned slowly, finally noticing Ben's computer monitor sitting on a small stand near his desk. "His computer is missing. Where's the CPU tower?"

"It's in the shop for repair. He was using his laptop for everything." Charlotte still regarded me thoughtfully.

"The rest of the rooms seems untouched. Could

you do a quick check and tell me if it appears that way to you, too?" Carter asked from the doorway.

"Sure. Charlotte, why don't you take upstairs and I'll do downstairs?" I passed her and went to the hallway, where Carter moved to one side so I could get by. I went into the kitchen, but the policeman was right. The dishwasher light showed green, telling me Ben had run the dishes and they waited to be removed and put away. I crossed the hall into the guest bedroom, but it appeared undisturbed as well.

I rejoined the officer in the front hallway. "Everything seems fine except for the living room and the study. His laptop is missing and some papers I gave him earlier today are gone. So are some notes he was making for a committee he and I serve on."

I gave Carter details about SOFT then Charlotte joined us. "I think everything is fine upstairs," she said. "I've never been there before, but nothing seemed unusual."

The master bedroom was upstairs, so apparently Ben and Charlotte hadn't progressed far enough in their relationship to use it. "Ben's very neat, so if everything looks okay, that means no one went in there," I said.

Carter nodded and shooed us out the door. I thankfully removed the latex gloves, which left a sweaty residue on my hands. "I'd like you both to come to the station tomorrow and make a statement about the missing papers," the officer said. "Mr. Raines should be able to give us more details, too."

We agreed to show up at the Manortown Police Department at nine in the morning, which was now just a few hours away. Carter drove off, and I walked with Charlotte to her car parked behind mine. "I'll see you in six hours," I said, glancing at my watch.

"Jane, do you really think someone attacked Ben to get those papers?"

"Yes, I do. It's the only thing missing—that and his committee notes. It has to have something to do with the road project."

"But who knew he had the papers? Besides me and you, that is." Charlotte unlocked her car and opened the driver's door.

I'd been considering that since Charlotte called me. "I can only think of two other people. Ann Burge and Luke Collins."

"That's ridiculous," Charlotte said immediately. "Ann couldn't attack Ben."

"But Luke could," I pointed out. "He's young and strong. I mean, I don't know for sure if he is, but he runs a ranch, so he must be strong, right?"

"But why would he hurt Ben?" Charlotte slid into her car. "He gave the papers to you in the first place. If he wanted them back, all he had to do was ask for them."

"It doesn't make sense," I agreed around a yawn. "I'm too tired to think about it now. I'll see you in a few hours."

"Do you want to stay at my house tonight?" she offered. "That way you don't have to drive back and forth."

"It's only ten miles. I'll be fine." I went to my car and got in, starting it and following Charlotte. I took a right turn and merged onto the two-lane highway that led back to Longbarn, my thoughts in a whirl.

Charlotte was right. If Luke wanted the papers back, he could ask for them. He had no reason to attack

Ben. It wasn't until I was almost home that I reasoned the only way Luke would know Ben had the papers was if Ann told him. Because Ann was there when I handed the papers over to Ben.

Good Lord, what a confusing mess. I got to my house and drove into the garage, closing the door behind me. I scurried into the house and checked the locks on the doors then I scrubbed my hands to get off the residue from those gloves. I set my alarm for seven-thirty, peeled off my clothes, and dropped into bed.

****

I awoke disoriented, wondering why my alarm went off. I always woke up before my buzzer. Then I remembered the hospital, the police, and what I had planned for the day.

I raced around my house getting ready. I had to go to the police station then stop at the Master Gardener office to meet Edie, who was in charge of the Garden Walk for the year. This was an annual fundraiser for the Master Gardener program where local private gardens allowed visitors for a nominal fee. Edie and I were visiting several local gardens to solicit volunteers. It was beautiful day for it, with fat puffy white clouds drifting through a pristine blue sky. Even the temperatures cooperated, and the humidity felt like it had dropped a dozen points or more.

I fed the cat and dashed out of the house, getting to Manortown in record time. Charlotte was already at the police station, waiting for me in the lobby. "Sorry I'm late," I said.

"No, I'm early. I went to the hospital to visit Ben before I came here." Charlotte turned to a woman sitting behind a metal desk positioned in front of a large doorway. "This is Miss Austin. You wanted to know when she arrived."

The woman nodded and went to the door, tapping in numbers on the combination lock before going inside. The door thudded shut behind her with solid finality.

"I should have cut some flowers for him, but I was in such a rush." I made a mental note to put together a bouquet for Ben and drop it off later in the day. "How's he doing? Did the doctor say when he can come home?"

"They're keeping him today, but Ben thought he might be released later this afternoon. I said I'd drive him home and make sure he got settled. I'll go over there after we're done here and make sure things get cleaned up. I recruited some students from his History 101 class to help me."

Good heavens. The woman was a dynamo of organization. I hadn't even considered his house and the shape it was in. She was right. "You've been a busy woman," I said. "I feel like a real slacker."

"I was just so keyed up when I got home I started making lists of things to do. I slept for a few hours then got up and figured I may as well get moving." She and I both turned when the door opened again, and the woman reappeared.

"This way," she said, going around the desk to another doorway, which led in turn to a hall. We were taken to a conference room where a stenographer and Officer Carter from the previous evening were waiting for us.

Charlotte and I gave our separate statements, her about the events of the evening, and me about the papers I had given Ben. Charlotte mentioned that Ben had made copies, but they were lost now, too. We were cautioned not to discuss details with anyone else and thirty minutes later we were leaving. Charlotte promised to call me as soon as she had any information about Ben's release from the hospital, then we each went our separate ways.

I met Edie at ten-thirty as planned, and she settled into the passenger seat, spreading a map open on her lap. "I've got it figured out," she said. "If we can get these houses lined up for Longbarn, then we could end the Garden Walk in Manortown. There are three gardens there that have potential."

"Did you tell anybody we were dropping by today?" I asked, following her directions to the north part of town.

"I checked to see if they'd be home, but I didn't go into detail why. I figured we'd just stop in and chat up the owners and maybe look the place over. I was afraid if I told them they were potential stops on the tour, they might turn me down flat. It's a lot harder to say no to somebody when they're standing in front of you, oohing and ahhing over your garden."

"Wise woman," I said with a grin.

She laughed and tilted her white straw hat to block the sunlight streaming into the car through the sunroof. Edie was a tiny woman in her forties who exuded energy and enthusiasm for whatever project she worked on. Her short-cropped blonde hair and small triangular face reminded me of a pixie or a mischievous elf, matching her mischievous personality. She and the other members of the Bossy Posse were indispensable in helping me hone my books for publication, and her sense of humor helped salve my wounded pride during some of our critique sessions.

I told her what happened to Ben but omitted the details about the stolen papers. "Crazy," she said with a disapproving shake of her head. "Why would someone break into his house? Did he have anything valuable to steal?"

"I don't think so," I said. "Wasn't it lucky that Charlotte lost her keys and came back to his house? Otherwise he might have gone into shock or bled to death or something."

"No kidding. Well, if that doesn't kickstart their relationship, I don't know what will." She grinned at me, familiar with Ben's indecisiveness when it came to women.

"You know, she said something like that. She talked about how she saw him lying there and she suddenly knew how she felt about him." I glanced at Edie, who had her head tilted up to the sunlight. "Do you think it really happens that way? Do you think people can suddenly see someone and realize they're in love?"

Edie nodded, her floppy hat waving gently with the movement. "Sometimes we just need the opportunity to see a person in a new light. After all, what do we really know about each other? We show different sides to different people. It's not often we get a chance to see the entire person, so to speak."

I mulled that over while we visited the Longbarn gardens on our stop. It was true that everyone had many facets to their lives. Look at me—teacher, committee member protesting the road construction, author, newspaper writer, and a gardener. Very few of my friends were familiar with every aspect of my life. In a way, friendships were like Venn diagrams, where people intersected in certain ways and didn't intersect in others.

And what about lovers? My marriage ended relatively quickly when I understood that I married not because of love, but because of loneliness. My ex-husband's affair with Ann only cemented the knowledge. That reminded me of Ben's problems and the fact that Ann was the only person who knew he had those papers. It seemed like every time I turned around, I fell over Ann Burge.

We stopped for lunch at a cafe in Manortown then went to the two gardens on Edie's list. One owner would be away during the tour, so we scratched that as a possibility. The other consented to take a spot, which left us with one more spot to fill. "I hope this one will be good," Edie said, giving me directions to a house on the northeast side of town. "It's an old garden but new owners, so it's hard to say if they'll want to be on the tour."

I parked in the driveway of a small Craftsman bungalow. Two maple trees dominated the front yard, and a paved walkway led around the house to the back through a pretty wooden arbor partially obscured by climbing wisteria which was in full bloom, a stunning display of lavender and pink.

We went to the front door and knocked, but there was no reply. I heard the rhythmic thunk of an axe coming from the back of the house. "Somebody must be chopping wood," I said.

"Let's check." Edie bustled along the pathway, going around the side of the house through the arbor and along the path flanked by a high row of flowering spirea. The heady scent of the bushes wafted around me, and I paused to take in a deep breath.

"Who is that?" Edie whispered.

I turned to see who she was staring at and did a double-take. A man stood near a downed tree at the back of the property, an axe in his hands. He was tackling a heap of large stumps and rows of stacked firewood attested to his efforts. His pale blue T-shirt stuck to his chest, showing off an impressive upper body and solidly muscled arms. The pale blue jeans he wore were just tight enough to highlight his cute butt and long legs. Curly gray hair, stubbled beard, and heavy work boots all combined with his torso to make him a vision of middle-aged male yumminess.

He turned, and I saw who it was.

"Be still my heart," Edie murmured. "Who's that?"

"Good God," I whispered. "Fitz."

Chapter 7

"That's the professor," I whispered in return. "Dr. Williams."

"Holy crap, he's a stud." Edie tilted her hat to a more rakish angle.

"You're married," I said chidingly. "And you're a lesbian."

"My hormones may not do a dance, but I can appreciate male beauty when I see it." Her pale blue eyes twinkled. "I guess we should have a chat, shouldn't we?"

"We should come back later. He's obviously busy."

"Nonsense. We're here, he's here, let's talk." Edie strode across the yard, a wide smile in place. I followed reluctantly, feeling like an intruder on the man's peaceful afternoon off.

Williams pulled away earbuds hooked into a small holder on his belt and let the buds dangle over his chest. "Hello, ladies. Can I help you?" He pulled an iPod from the holder and pressed a button on it.

Edie surged forward, hand outstretched. "I'm Edie Knight, president of the Derby County Garden Society. I spoke to you earlier today. We're checking on gardens for our Garden Walk, and we were told you have some of the finest gardens in the county."

Williams leaned his axe against a stump and wiped

his hands on his jeans before shaking her hand. "I'm afraid my garden isn't worthy of a tour. It was overgrown when I bought the house and it's a work in progress." He glanced at me. "Hello, Miss Austin. I should have known you were interested in gardening. The flower beds at your house are very nice."

"They don't call her Nature Girl for nothing," Edie gushed. "You've read her articles in the paper, haven't you? Of course, you have, you did a critique of our local writers, didn't you? They're such marvelous articles, aren't they? So humorous and they capture the flavor of country living so well."

Williams twisted to tuck the iPod back into its holder. When he straightened, his brown eyes held a hint of accusation when he regarded me. "I didn't know Miss Austin and Nature Girl were one and the same. That must be one of those town secrets I'm not privy to." His frosty look thawed. "I heard what happened to Ben. Do the police have any idea who did it?"

"Why ask me?" I tried to appear innocent.

He smiled, dimples appearing at the sides of his mouth. "Charlotte told me that you and she were at the police station. Since you seem to be involved in everything in town, I thought you might know."

"You give me too much credit." I walked past him, acutely aware that he was watching me. I wished I'd worn something nicer than a pair of jeans and my short-sleeved blue top.

"The garden was neglected for years. The lady who lived here was unable to care for it," he said behind me.

"I can see the structure, though." I walked onto a narrow, mulched path that wound its way into a series of five distinct flower beds. They were set in a semicircle and partially surrounded a small lawn. Old oaks and beech trees bordered it on the north. A spirea hedge on the west side matched the one on the east side we passed when we walked in.

"That's one of the herb gardens," he said behind me. "Or it will be once I get it under control." I turned. Williams was behind me, pointing to the second flower bed. I continued to wander, drinking in the riot of color and texture in the center bed.

"There is a design." His voice was very close behind me. I looked back and he moved forward, so close I felt his warmth. "The outermost beds are low-growing perennials. The next in are herbs, and here in the middle are prairie flowers." He pointed to a swatch of coneflowers swaying in the breeze. "I had to do a lot of studying to figure out what I had." He peered into my eyes, just a few inches away. "Perhaps I should ask Nature Girl to give me a hand, identifying what's in the beds." One corner of his mouth quirked up in half-smile.

I stared up at him, lost in the depths of his brown eyes. "I'd be glad to help," I murmured inanely.

He smiled at Edie, who had paused next to the herb garden. "I'm afraid this doesn't deserve to be on your garden tour."

Edie regarded me then Williams then me again. "I, I mean, we, that is, the Society, well, this would be just perfect. A work in progress. We can call it a reclamation project. The tour isn't difficult. It's only one afternoon. One of our volunteers will help you get ready for it. It's a fundraiser for the Garden Society, and enables us to—"

"Are you a volunteer for the tour?" Williams

asked, moving closer to me.

I wanted to step back but I saw nowhere to go without being obvious. "Yes, I am," I said, looking anywhere but at him. I ended up focusing on a sweaty spot on his chest and reluctantly raised my eyes to his. "I usually handle publicity and often help at different homes."

"If you don't object, we could tour this year and next, to see what changes you've made." Edie beamed at him then me, eyes twinkling with mischief. "That would give us a nice feeling for what goes into such a restoration attempt. I'm sure Jane would love to help, wouldn't you, Jane?"

"Then I accept," Williams said. "Miss Austin can help me get ready for the tour and fill me in on any nuances for the event."

"Of course. I'd be glad to help." I forced a smile at Edie and at Williams then turned to go back the way we came. "We'll be in touch. The tour will be in three weeks."

"I told Charlotte I'd stay with Ben and help him if he needs it."

I turned around slowly. "Really?"

"Apparently there is some concern that he might need help around the house, at least temporarily. Charlotte and I can take turns helping him if needed."

"That's very good of you, Dr. Williams." Edie jotted a note in her garden notebook. "I'm surprised his family isn't stepping in to help."

"I'm not." "I'm not."

Williams and I spoke simultaneously. "Great minds think alike, apparently," Edie murmured, walking back toward the front of the house.

"If you knew his family, you'd know why we say that." I started after her, but my foot slipped on a paver in the path. I twisted, trying to catch my balance.

Williams put a hand under my arm to steady me. "I can see I have some repairs to do if people will be walking through my yard," he said. "Are you okay?"

"Yes, I'm fine. Just clumsy of me." I moved away from him, but he kept pace beside me, walking so close his arm brushed mine while I followed Edie.

"You'll have to come over and help me decide what's needed to prepare for the tour," Williams said. "I'll need your advice, I'm sure."

"I didn't know you knew Ben's family," Edie commented, her voice carefully neutral.

"I know his brother-in-law," Williams said. "A most disagreeable person, wouldn't you say, Miss Austin?"

"Very. And please, call me Jane. After all, we'll be working together." I was surprised to see startled pleasure in his eyes. "No need to be so formal."

"And you have to reciprocate and call me Fitz. Does that mean you forgive me?" he asked, pausing at the arbor separating the back yard from the front.

I turned so my back was to Edie. "I'm considering it," I said softly, examining the dense blossoms swaying above us. "This is an amazing plant. It must be decades old to be so thick and full."

"I can't take credit for it. I inherited it with the house." He peered beyond me to Edie. "I'm looking forward to the garden tour. I'm sure Jane can give me some excellent ideas for improvement." He smiled. "In my garden, that is."

I laughed. "I'm sure I can."

115

"Why don't we plan a celebratory dinner tonight?"

"Celebratory?" I walked slowly through the arbor, savoring the foliage surrounding me.

"To celebrate Ben's release from the hospital, of course." Fitz touched a small plaster Buddha tucked into a niche of the arbor. "I'm meeting Charlotte at the hospital at four to get Ben. We'll get him settled then perhaps we can have a quiet meal together. Why don't you come over to his house at five? Charlotte and I will fix dinner, and you can bring dessert and wine. Unless you're busy with classes?"

"No, I'm teaching Monday, Wednesday, Friday this summer."

"So am I. Another thing we have in common." He swept his hand downward at his dirty clothes. "That explains my ensemble for today. Had I known you were coming, I would have changed."

"That's perfectly fine for yardwork." I stopped by my car door. "I have a special outfit I wear when I garden, too."

"We'll have to get together sometime and compare style."

I thought of my disreputable ragged T-shirt and shorts that I wore when gardening. "I don't think 'style' is the correct term. Thank you for helping with Ben," I said. "I'm sure he appreciates it."

"He's been very welcoming to me since I moved here. I'm happy to repay the favor." Williams tapped my car. "I considered getting a Mini. I rather wish I had."

"If you'd like to take a test drive sometime, just let me know." I slipped behind the wheel. "I'm always happy to make converts."

He leaned over to peer at Edie then me. "Good to know. Please keep me in the loop about the tour, Mrs. Knight." He straightened while I backed the car up and watched us drive away. I glanced in the rear-view mirror and he was still watching. Then he waved once and went into the house.

"He seems like an amazingly pleasant man," Edie said.

"I know. I'm surprised." I was busy trying to fit the easy-going Fitz Williams with my mental image of Dr. Williams, arrogant jerk.

"Why do you say that?"

"The last few times he and I spoke, he was a bit high-handed. Almost arrogant."

"Perhaps it was the company he keeps. Was someone with him when you two spoke?"

I thought about it. The only extended conversation Fitz Williams and I had was interrupted by George Wicks. "Yes, I guess you could say that."

"Well, you can't judge a person based on a few conversations. I suspect Mr. Williams has hidden depths that you know nothing about." Edie regarded me. "Although I think you'll find out sooner rather than later. The gentleman is interested in you."

I waved a hand. "A fellow professor, that's all."

"Hmm. Maybe." She smiled smugly "Perhaps there's a romance in your future."

"Oh, please."

She waggled a finger at me. "Trust me, dear. The gentleman is interested."

I diverted her attention by reviewing the gardens we visited that day and soon dropped her off at her house. I called Charlotte when I got home. "I spoke with Fitz Williams today. He told me he's helping with Ben."

"Yes, I talked to him. He mentioned you're coming to dinner tonight. I think it's a marvelous idea. Ben is anxious to talk to you about the files he scanned. And Fitz is anxious to make a good impression on you."

"I barely know the man. I doubt he's that anxious." I wasn't sure what to say. Fitz Williams' interest in me was a mystery.

"Look, I may be speaking out of turn, but I think you should understand his background. He's always been pressured to do the right thing, to do what's expected of a son in his family. I told you his people are big wigs, right? They're socially connected and behind-the-scene shakers in politics. Fitz's father was bitterly disappointed when Fitz only practiced law for a few years."

I forgot that interesting tidbit. Was that why he pressed George Wick the other night about the difference between an attorney and a lawyer? "How did he become a college professor?"

"That's just it. Fitz worked in his father's law firm for more than ten years, but he was miserable. He was engaged to a girl, but she was after his name and his money and his position in society. When Fitz told her that he wanted to go back to school and get a degree in English Literature, she dumped him. Then his family dumped him. Well, metaphorically speaking they did, I guess. He was cut off without a penny, which of course wasn't too bad since he had already made a bundle on the stock market and invested it."

"Good heavens, it sounds like something out a Victorian novel." I contrasted Fitz Williams' background with my own. My parents were mildly eccentric, borderline poor, and unfailingly supportive of my desire to make a living as a teacher. After their deaths I was astonished to discover they had saved thousands of dollars and left it to me, which enabled me to weather the disastrous scandal at Derby College.

"It's just a generational thing. I guess you have to be from there to understand it. Fitz and his parents finally made peace of sorts, but I think they were a bit ashamed of him. When he came here, Ann Burge immediately latched herself onto him, and it was like the past had come back to haunt him. Here was this woman who was attracted to his money and his connections. Then he met you, and you don't give a rip about any of that."

I laughed. "I didn't even know about any of that. But you're right, I don't give a rip."

"That's what's so great for him. This is his chance to finally branch out and do what he wants to do without his family right at his shoulder. They used to hate that he wanted to actually do the work in his garden, for example." Charlotte's voice took on a snooty, nasal quality. "Get your hands dirty? Why don't you hire it done?"

"Where's the fun in that?" I asked. "Half the fun of gardening is kicking back and having a cold beer once you're done with the sweaty work."

"You know that, and Fitz knows that, but his family sure didn't. Anyway, I just wanted you to know where he's coming from. It's a tough adjustment for him because he's always been held to extremely high standards."

"What you're saying is he has to learn to be

humble," I said wryly.

"What I meant is he's always been humble, but he's never been allowed to show it. So just give him a chance, okay? He's one of the best people I know. I think you and he would make a great couple."

Couple of what? I almost said, but I didn't. "I'll take your words under advisement," I promised. "I'll see you in a few hours."

"Okay. Thanks, Jane."

"For what? You and Fitz Williams are doing all the work."

"Thanks for encouraging me to tell Ben how I feel. I told him this morning and, well, I think you're right. I think he cares for me, too."

I laughed again. "Charlotte, he's head over heels in love with you."

"I know. Isn't it great?" She sounded as dreamy as any love-sick teenager. "Have to go now. I'll see you soon."

If Ben was as besotted as she was, he probably didn't mind a mild concussion and broken ribs. I'll bet he didn't even feel it. Ah, love, I thought. I pulled two bottles of wine from my cooler then began to make chocolate sauce for the ice cream I would buy on the way to Ben's house.

As I cooked I considered my conversations with Charlotte and Edie. Maybe they were right. Maybe I was guilty of hasty judgement where Fitz Williams was concerned. My previous marriage and subsequent divorce had left me cynical about relationships. Perhaps it was time to open myself up to new possibilities. My few relationships post-divorce were amiable but not particularly passionate or involving. I had the feeling

Fitz Williams would not settle for a merely amiable relationship.

Something to consider.

I dressed with care, choosing my nicest pair of black capris, strappy sandals, and a flowing pastel cotton top that was cool and comfortable. Just as I was leaving, my phone rang. It was Luke Collins.

"I heard that my father's papers were stolen."

"How did you hear that?" I juggled the phone while I packed a canvas bag with wine and chocolate sauce.

"Ann mentioned it. She and I were talking. She said you gave the papers to someone and he was robbed. Is that true?"

"Yes, I gave them to a friend of mine on the SOFT committee. Ben is a local historian, and I was hoping he could find something that would help us."

"That's too bad. My father really wanted you to have those files." He sounded genuinely unhappy about the loss of the documents. "Ann and I were talking with George Wick about them yesterday. George was interested, too, in their historical value."

It was hard to believe George Wick had any concern about historical documents, but perhaps George had depths I didn't know. Or maybe Luke was wrong. Whatever. I considered telling Luke that Ben had scanned most of the papers but remembered in time that I wasn't supposed to share that knowledge. Of course, it was a moot point because Ben's laptop was stolen, too. "Perhaps the police will recover them," I said doubtfully.

"Perhaps. Well, if I can help in any way, let me know. I skimmed through the files before I gave them to you, so if the police need an inventory, I might be able to help."

"I'm seeing Ben tonight and I'll mention that. In fact, I need to get going or I'll be late." I glanced at my watch as though that action would speed him up.

"Oh. Well, let me know if I can help." He seemed reluctant to end the conversation.

I decided to do it for him. "Will do." I hung up the phone and headed out. I stopped for ice cream then got stuck in a bit of traffic so it was after five o'clock when I arrived. I knocked and Charlotte called, "Come in."

I entered and nearly dropped my satchel in shock. The house looked like it had never been ransacked. Charlotte and Ben sat in the living room on my left, cocktails on the coffee table in front of them. "Wow," I said. "You must have hired miracle workers, Charlotte."

"Never underestimate the energy of an undergraduate student," Ben said. He moved carefully when he leaned forward to pick up his glass.

Charlotte got to her feet, handed him his glass, and then came to me. "The kids worked all morning. Heck, they didn't have class and most of them were happy to help. Fitz is out back, getting coals ready to barbeque steaks."

"I have ice cream and hot fudge sauce," I said, holding up my bag. "And two bottles of wine."

"I'll put it away for you," Charlotte offered. "The fridge is packed full of food. I swear everybody on the faculty brought over a hot dish."

"Except for the guys in the Philosophy Department," Ben said with a small chuckle. "They brought over a case of beer."

"Wise men." I handed my bag to Charlotte and went into the living room. "How are you doing? Does it hurt a bunch?"

"Only if I move quickly. I've got a couple of broken ribs but otherwise I'm fine. I had a headache most of the night, but that's gone now." He glanced down the hall where Charlotte had gone. "I feel almost okay."

I smiled. "I think you have more than restored health to credit your happy mood."

He smiled. "I guess it was worth getting beat up if it helps me get the girl."

"Don't you dare say that." I leaned over and kissed his cheek. "I'm so glad you're okay. You looked like crap last night. Do the police have any leads? Did you hear from them today?"

"Let's talk about it over dinner," Charlotte said from the hall. "That way Ben doesn't have to repeat everything twice. Ben, why don't we move into the kitchen? That's where the action will be."

I helped him to his feet and held his arm to walk down the hall, Charlotte following behind us with their drinks. I got Ben into a chair at the kitchen nook then I fixed myself a drink and went through the sliding door to the deck where Fitz Williams sat in a lawn chair, a round black barbeque grill nearby. He had changed from his work clothes to sandals, khaki shorts, and a dark brown polo shirt, all of which accented his golden tan.

"I heard you're in charge of the fire," I said.

"I only hope my cooking does justice to the steaks Charlotte brought."

I took the seat next to him. "It was scary last night

at the hospital. And I didn't even see the worst of it. Charlotte was the one who stopped the bleeding and got him help. She's an amazing woman."

Fitz nodded. "I've known her most of my life. Her father and my father worked in the same law firm. Our families often took holidays together at the shore."

"It sounds like something in a movie. My family's idea of a holiday was to throw the family in the car and go camping at the state park for the weekend."

Fitz sipped his drink then got up to check the grill. "My father's idea of a holiday was to throw us in the car then he went back to the city to work. I'm not complaining, though. He was only really happy when he was working, and it was often uncomfortable to have him around when he tried so hard to relax."

Charlotte stepped out of the house, a covered plate in her hands. "As per your instructions, the steaks have rested for an hour. Are the coals ready?"

He gave her a mock salute. "Yes, sir. Ready when you are."

She set the tray on the plastic table between the lawn chairs. "I'll leave you two in charge and I'll get the asparagus ready."

"Anything I can do to help?" I asked.

"Just keep an eye on Fitz and make sure he doesn't mess up those steaks," Ben called from the kitchen.

Charlotte laughed and went back inside. I glimpsed her leaning over Ben, then the angle of sun on the sliding door obscured them. When I turned back to Fitz, he was watching me. "It appears they've resolved their hesitation," he said softly.

I picked up the plate and uncovered two Porterhouse steaks. "I think a near-death experience can change a lot of things."

"I'm happy for Charlotte. She's a great friend and she's had a few relationships that weren't right for her."

"In what way?"

Fitz used the tongs to put the steaks on the grill. "The men weren't good enough for her. I think she was settling, you know?" He glanced at me then adjusted the steaks with small taps. "I think there's a point in life when people think they need to be part of a pair, and they're willing to compromise too much to make that happen."

I thought ruefully of my marriage. I got married when I was twenty-eight and had that panicked feeling that life was passing me by. It took me ten years to know I was far happier alone than with a man I didn't respect. "I can understand that," I murmured.

"At first I thought Ben was something of a slacker. I thought that about a lot of people at Derby, I suppose, because it's a small college and away from the mainstream. It took me awhile to see that the focus here is on teaching and on community involvement. Student evaluations are taken very seriously. And most of the faculty are involved in some kind of volunteer work in addition to their coursework. Some professors work as tutors. Another one I know is helping a non-profit organization write grants." He stepped back, his cheeks flushed from the heat. "And you write articles for the local newspaper."

"That reminds me. What do you think of Nature Girl?" I asked off-handedly. "Joan mentioned you were going to evaluate our regular columnists."

"I think Nature Girl has a fresh, original, and witty voice. I think she's very charming, independent, often opinionated, talented, and very pretty." He sipped his drink, watching my reaction over the rim of his glass.

"You can tell that by reading an article or two?" I sipped my drink, too, using it to give me time to gather my scattered thoughts. "How do you reconcile your opinion of Nature Girl with your opinion of Jane Austin, romance author?"

"That's a subject that will require a great deal of in-depth thought. I expect I'll need to do a bit more research and perhaps have private interviews in order to come to any fresh conclusion. That is, of course, if you're willing to engage in any discussions." He moved closer to me, so close I caught a whiff of a faint sage scent. "I still say your heroine was too naive to be believable."

"And I still say you didn't evaluate the arc of the entire book." I looked up at him. "But I concede that if you didn't notice how she changed, then perhaps I did fail to portray her personality completely. I hope I do better in the next two books."

"How long did it take you to write the first book?"

"About six months. I'm just about done with the second one, but I think I need some brainstorming for the third book. I can't wrap up the trilogy the way I wanted."

"What's the problem?" He moved forward to nudge the steaks with the tongs, brushing against my arm when he did.

"The overall arc for the trilogy is the reversal of personal traits. She starts as uncertain and immature and ends up being the one who takes command. The hero starts as arrogant and self-confident but then he's put into a position where he has to rely on her. The problem is I have them in a situation where I'm not sure she can assume the lead."

"Hmm. You're right. Some brainstorming might be in order." His dark brown eyes were warm and inviting. "Maybe tomorrow night, at my house? You can give me some gardening advice, and perhaps I can help you with plot advice."

Common sense warred with flirtation. Common sense won. "You'd better keep an eye on those steaks or Charlotte will yell at you." I moved away, back to the house. "I'll go see if I can help her with anything." I went inside, overheated from more than just the barbeque. It was a long time since an attractive—no, a sexy—man flirted with me, and I was badly out of practice. I needed some time to decide how to handle the situation.

We ate on the deck under the awning Ben extended. He repeated his story of the break-in then said, "I doubt the police will ever find those documents. I've been thinking about it. If someone stole them, they won't keep them because that would be evidence of the crime. Whoever did it will most likely destroy the files."

"You said you scanned in the files, though, right? Maybe if the police find your laptop, we can get the copies back." I leaned back in my chair, replete with the meal.

"I have copies whether they get the machine back or not." Ben smiled wryly. "I lost a lot of work once when I had a hard disk crash, so now I back up everything. I have an online backup service that copies everything automatically. You know what I mean. It's a cloud thing where backups are done in the background.

Plus I have an external hard drive hooked to my laptop."

"So everything is copied?" I asked.

"Twice. Like I said, I'm the king of paranoid when it comes to computers." Ben shrugged then winced when his broken ribs protested. "All it takes is one hard disk meltdown and you'd be paranoid, too."

I thought of my novels-in-progress and knew what he meant. I had a similar online backup service, but maybe I should get an external drive, too. "You can't have too many backups. Where is it? The backup drive?" I asked, getting up from the table.

"I always had it hooked to a cord and tucked under my chair. It might still be there." Ben looked at Charlotte.

"The students who cleaned up put everything back on shelves. They didn't mention a backup hard drive."

Fitz stood, too. "I'll help you find it. I brought a spare laptop for Ben to use until his computer gets back from the shop."

I hesitated, not sure it was a wise idea to be alone with him. I didn't see a graceful way to avoid it, though, and really, what did it matter? I had to interact with the man, right?

He and I went into the house. "Charlotte said his laptop was in the living room, so that's where the drive should be. When I got here last night, the end table and the chair were both tipped over." I went to the corner where I'd searched that night for Ben's laptop. The chair had been righted and the broken lamp moved to the far side of the room, leaving the remaining working lamp next to the chair.

"I'll check the bookcases," Fitz said. "Maybe a

student found it and set it on a shelf."

"I wonder if they vacuumed," I said as I got on my hands and knees and inched forward on the wood floor. "It's clean. There was some broken glass here earlier."

"Charlotte said they took the area rug and cleaned it outside then swept the floors. I think they were pressed for time."

"I still say they were miracle workers. This place was a mess last night." I peered under the TV stand, using that vantage point to peek under the couch and Ben's chair. I was about ready to give up when I shifted position and spied something.

"Eureka." I sat back on my heels and held up the hard rectangular drive. It was about as big as a mini-tablet but totally black. "I'll bet whoever took the laptop thought this was part of the power cord or something."

Fitz held out his hand and pulled me to my feet. When I started to move away, he held me still. "Jane, I think you're a woman with an appreciation of the sensibilities of others. If my attention is unwanted, please tell me now and I'll leave you alone and quit bothering you. I'll be happy to have you help me with the garden tour, but I won't pester you with my interest." He stared into my eyes, pinning me with his gaze.

I started to stammer some inane reply but his honesty forced honesty from me. "It's been a long time since a man expressed any sort of romantic interest in me." I blushed but plowed on. "I thought I had reached an age of life where that sort of thing wouldn't happen to me. I thought it was reserved for younger people."

He arched an eyebrow. "Like the heroine in your

book, perhaps? I don't believe age is a predictor of romantic inclination. I admire your intellect, I applaud your tenacity, and I think you're a damn attractive woman. If you want me to leave you alone, then—"

I dropped the drive in the chair, stepped forward, put my hands on his shoulders, and drew him closer to me. "I want you to kiss me."

Chapter 8

We both were hesitant, unsure. Then I stepped closer, or maybe he did. I felt him against me and somehow we melted against each other. I twined my arms around his neck and sank into his embrace. Long forgotten emotions, sensations, excitements began to pulse in me. When we finally pulled apart, I was dizzy with anticipation.

"Eureka," I whispered.

Fitz slowly ran his hand over the side of my face, gently tracing the line of my chin while he stared into my eyes. "I'm glad you decided to give me another chance."

"I confess," I said, smiling up at him. "It was your garden that sealed the deal."

"I told you. It's a work in progress." He kissed the tip of my nose. "As am I. It's been a long time since I cared for anyone. Please be patient."

"I know how you feel. It's been a long time for me, too." I pulled him to me for a brief, lingering kiss. "We'll be patient with each other."

"Did you find it?" Charlotte called from the dining room.

"I think so," I called back. I moved away from Fitz to the hallway but he held onto my hand, stopping me.

"My house, tomorrow night?" he asked softly.

I nodded and slipped away from him, heading for

the hallway. Charlotte met us mid-way. "Where's the laptop you brought Ben to use?" I asked Fitz.

"I put it in the study." He took the backup drive from me and went into Ben's office. I started to follow but Charlotte put a hand on my arm.

"Ben's going to rest for a while in the spare room," she said in a low voice. "You two see what you can find on the drive. I'll clean up in the kitchen."

"I can help." I glanced into the study. "We'll be back in a minute."

Fitz looked up from Ben's desk where he was leaning over an open laptop. "I'll see if I can access the files on the drive."

I joined Charlotte in the kitchen. "Ben isn't overdoing it, is he?" I started stacking dishes into the dishwasher, being as quiet as I could since the spare room where Ben was resting was just across the hall.

"I think the pain pills they gave him make him tired, that's all. Fitz is staying here tonight in case Ben needs help. I know Ben is anxious to have Fitz check those documents. He wanted to get Fitz's legal opinion about some of them." Charlotte bustled around the kitchen, putting away leftovers.

"You know, with the excitement about Ben, I forgot to ask about Mr. Collins. Did they discover the cause of death yet? I wonder when his funeral will be. I should have asked Luke Collins about it today when he called."

"What did he want?"

"He heard from Ann that his father's papers were stolen. I suppose he was curious about what happened."

"The last I heard, his death was still being called an accident. There isn't any reason to think otherwise, really." Charlotte studied the now-tidy kitchen. "This is a pretty little house, isn't it? Ben said he's lived here for ten years."

"It suits you just fine," I said teasingly.

"That's not what I meant, but thank you." Charlotte looked past me, to the hall. "Fitz has rather a nice house, too, doesn't he?"

I saw the knowing expression in her eyes and I had to grin. "Yes, he does. I had a tour of his garden recently and I'll have a chance to see the inside tomorrow night. We're having dinner at his house."

Charlotte was so pleased I thought she might burst. "That's marvelous. I just know you're a match made in heaven. You're perfect for each other."

I did laugh at that. "I'm having dinner at his house, we're not eloping."

"Oh, you know what I mean. I'm so pleased you've put your differences aside. This is the start of a beautiful relationship, I just know it. I never thought Fitz and Ann were a good fit."

Ann Burge. I had forgotten about her and Fitz. She and I had an acrimonious relationship to start with. When she discovered Fitz and I were seeing each other, she'd probably come after me with guns blazing. "How long have they been dating?"

"Off and on for a few months. Since the first of the year, I guess. I don't think it ever really went anywhere. I mean, I think it was mostly one-sided, on Ann's part. It was convenient for Fitz to have someone to go to faculty events with him, and since Ann is on the faculty, it just sort of worked out."

That gave me a pang. If he and I started dating, we might have to attend social functions at Derby. I had mostly avoided my old alma mater despite my exoneration and a subsequent apology from the department chairman. I gave a mental shrug. That was a bridge I'd cross at some point if I had to. "I was surprised to see her with him at the town meeting the other night. I know her mother is adamantly opposed to the road construction project, and she was there with Fitz, who is in favor of it." I frowned. "I'll need to talk to him about that."

"I don't think Ann has any strong opinions either way. She strikes me as the kind of person who agrees with whoever is in the room at the time." Charlotte grinned. "Is it obvious I don't like her?"

"I would never have guessed," I dead-panned.

Laughing, we left the kitchen. "Let's see if Fitz managed to get those files loaded," Charlotte said, leading the way to the study. "I'm so excited. Maybe we'll be able to recover them after all. I know Ben felt so bad that they were stolen. He felt responsible for them."

"For heaven's sake, it's not his fault they were taken."

"I know, but they were in his care. I suppose you wouldn't understand unless you were an historian, like us. Having old documents like that is like a gold mine. It can tell us so much."

Fitz sat at Ben's big desk, the laptop open in front of him. The backup hard drive was attached via a USB cable to one of the ports on the laptop.

"Were you able to recover any files?" I asked, coming around the desk to peer down at the computer. Several documents were open on the screen. "Wow. You did it."

"I can't take any credit. His backup drive is plug-and-play. I plugged it in and it installed the necessary software. I just followed a few prompts and was able to get at the files he worked on last. He scanned about forty documents. Does that sound right to you?"

"I think there were more files than that." I glanced at Charlotte. "Did he scan everything?"

She came around the desk on Fitz's other side. "He scanned the ones he thought might have legal implications. The others seemed like personal documents or diaries and he only scanned a few of those. He planned to go through them later."

"If it's okay with you, Jane, I'll make copies of these." Fitz pulled a small memory stick from his shirt pocket. "Ben asked me to review them for any legal problems I might see."

"They aren't mine," I said. "Mr. Collins left them to the committee. I'm sure it's okay. Was Ben hoping to find something that might help us?"

"Ben did," Ben said from the doorway. "I know Fitz has a legal background. I scanned in the documents that appeared to have something to do with the land purchase or sale." He came into the room, yawning. "I'm sorry to be such a party-pooper."

"Don't be silly." I helped him to the armchair next to the desk. "You're still recovering. I should go and let you get some real rest."

He smiled sheepishly and ran a hand through his curly hair, which was even more untidy than usual. "I must be getting old. A couple of busted ribs and I'm down for the count."

"I'd be down for more than the count." I hugged him carefully, making sure not to jostle him too much.

"Don't fret yourself about the files. Who knows? Maybe the police will catch whoever did it." He started to get up but I gently pushed him back into the chair. "You sit down. I can let myself out."

Fitz came around the desk. "I'll walk with you to your car."

Charlotte met us at the door to the hall. "Thanks for coming over and bringing that awesome dessert." She hugged me again and this time I was ready for her enthusiasm.

"Glad to do it. Let me know if anything comes up I can help with." I went to the kitchen for my satchel and purse then Fitz and I walked to my car.

"Why don't you come over to my house at six tomorrow night," Fitz suggested, pausing by my driver's door.

I tossed my bags into the car then turned to him. His arms went around me and I leaned back against the car. "Six o'clock tomorrow sounds fine," I said. "Shall I bring dessert again?"

He pressed against me. "I have other ideas for dessert."

The kiss this time was much less hesitant and much more insistent. By the time we separated, I was definitely feeling overheated. I reluctantly slipped into the car and buckled up. "Thanks for helping with Ben," I said through the open window. "And for going through those files. I know he was worried about them."

"Like I said, I'm glad to help." He touched my cheek gently. "I'm starting to feel at home here."

"Good." I drove away slowly, watching him in my rearview mirror as he watched me. Then he went back to the house and I drove home, feeling like I was floating on Cloud Nine. It was a couple of years since I had a man in my life, and it was even longer since I had a man like Fitz Williams—someone intelligent, sexy, and handsome.

My euphoric feeling lasted through the night, and I awoke feeling happy and anxious to face my day. So what if I had classes to teach and papers to grade and a chapter to write? I'd manage to get it done and still get to Fitz's house by six. I felt like I could handle anything thrown at me.

As I went about my usual Wednesday, I was surprised how my perspective had changed. True, Fitz had come across as arrogant and a bit condescending at first, but now I knew him better and I understood some of his background. I could put his actions and comments into context, as it were. Like me, he had a less than happy brush with romance, and like me, he had an unhappy career path.

A niggling voice in the back of my head wondered about his wealthy family and whether they still exerted any influence on him. And a small, nagging worry made me think about Ann and how she would feel when she knew Fitz and I were seeing each other. I pushed those worries to one side and decided to enjoy the moment while I could.

The blissful ignorance lasted through my day teaching class and into the afternoon. I was at home and working in fits and starts on a chapter in my novel when my phone rang. "Hey, Ben," I said when I answered, recognizing the phone number. "How are you doing?"

"Pretty good. I slept through the night and into the

morning. Fitz stayed last night with me, and Charlotte was here when I woke up." He laughed softly. "It's nice waking up to a good breakfast, fresh coffee, and a smiling face."

"See what you've been missing," I teased. "I told you that you were a slowpoke and you needed to let her know how you felt."

"As soon as I feel better I'll make up for lost time. I'll tell you, there's nothing like a life-changing event to make you realize what's missing in your life. Charlotte said you and Fitz hit it off pretty good." His cheerful tone shifted to one of doubt.

"We did. Why? Any reason we shouldn't have?"

"Well, I'm not sure. It's just that Fitz spent most of the night going through those files we recovered on my backup disk."

"He said he was going to try to evaluate some of them. Isn't that what you wanted him to do? I thought you said there were some legal documents there that you wanted a lawyer to examine. Or an attorney. Or somebody who knows about the law," I said, not sure which was which. Was Fitz an attorney or a lawyer? I couldn't remember.

"Yeah, I did. It's just, well…" His voice trailed away.

"Come on, Ben. Spit it out. You've got something to tell me, right?" I stared at my computer screen, frowning at a run-on sentence that needed fixing.

"I think Fitz deleted some files."

My attention riveted back on the phone. "What? Why do you say that?"

"I told you I use an online backup program in addition to the backup drive. I checked my files online and compared them to the ones Fitz recovered. They're different."

"Different how?"

"When I scanned the documents into my computer, I let the scan program just number them for me. I didn't bother giving them names because I wasn't sure what the files were."

"Okay," I said, visualizing what he was talking about. "So?"

"So a lot of them are missing. For example, I have scans numbered thirty through forty in the online backup directory but they're missing on the backup drive."

"Missing?"

"Fitz was the only one who handled that backup drive. He copied the directory I set up onto the laptop he brought me and I compared that directory to the one that's in the online backup directory. They're different."

"Did you ask him about it?"

"I tried. I mean, I called his office but…"

"But what?"

"Well, he and Ann usually have lunch together, and I called his office about a half-hour ago and Ann answered. She sort of laughed and said he was busy then she hung up. I—that's why I called you because— I wasn't sure if he and Ann—I mean, I think he and Ann are—I mean, I wasn't sure if you—"

Don't jump to conclusions, I told myself. Maybe Fitz wasn't even there. Maybe Ann answered his phone and decided to act like a bitch and mess with Ben. It was the kind of thing she'd do. But that little niggling voice started talking more loudly in my head while my stomach started to churn. Fitz and Ann lunched together every day? That sounded like a *relationship* to me, despite what Fitz claimed.

"I'm supposed to see him tonight. I can ask him, I suppose." *If I see him,* that niggling voice whispered. *Maybe you don't want to get involved with him if he's acting like a shit.* "Did you mention this to Charlotte? Maybe she and Fitz talked about the files." Charlotte had said that Fitz didn't care for Ann. Maybe they were closer than she thought. *Stop it,* I whispered to myself. *Don't assume the worst. Don't assume he's sleeping with her even though she is younger and thinner and more like him, stylish and polished and rich.*

I pushed away from my desk and got up to pace my office. As I did, I knocked off the stack of mail still piled there, waiting for my attention. The note from Mr. Collins fluttered to the floor, the spidery script so elegant and flowing.

"I'll ask her tonight," Ben said. "She's coming for dinner. I just wanted you to know—I mean, I don't want you to be hurt. If he's lying about the files, or if he's still with Ann then I thought I should tell you and—"

"It's okay." Poor Ben sounded panicked, and I could imagine him, broken ribs and all, anxiously doing what I was doing, pacing around his office. "You sit down and rest. Don't worry about this. I'm sure there's a reasonable explanation for everything."

"I hope so, Jane. I like him and he's Charlotte's friend. It would be really bad if he was an asshole and I had to hate him."

I laughed in spite of the dread creeping over me. "You won't have to hate him because of me," I assured him. "There's nothing between us, so if he and Ann are having a fling in his office, it won't hurt me at all." *Liar, liar, liar,* the little voice shouted.

"Oh, man, I'm so glad to hear you say that. I was afraid, well, you know. After what happened with Tommy and Ann and the whole stupid thing ten years ago, it would be the last straw if Ann pulled her shit again on you." Ben sounded so relieved that I was determined to make sure he believed me.

"Don't fret. I'm more worried about those files that might be missing." I went to my desk and stared down at my SOFT notebook, the small turtle stickers interspersed with flowers and other greenery on the cover. I noticed pages sticking from it. I still had Mr. Collin's notes about the history of the subdivision. I pulled them out and laid them on top of the mail stack.

"I'll talk to Charlotte about it tonight. She said you and Fitz were having dinner together. Maybe you can ask him."

"I think it would be better if you asked him," I said. "You know the details, after all. I just know the general outline, so to speak."

"Oh, yeah. Sure. I'll talk to Charlotte then I'll give him a call. Tomorrow, maybe. I'm sure it's nothing important." There was a pause. "I'd better go now. Charlotte's coming over in a few minutes and I need to get cleaned up. I just wanted you to know."

"Thanks, Ben. You guys have fun tonight, and take it easy. You're still wounded, remember? Say hi to Charlotte for me." I hung up before he could fumble another apology.

I walked to the French doors and stared at the birds fluttering around the feeders beyond my porch. Ann and Fitz were in his office, having a quickie. That's what it sounded like, at least. *They always have lunch together.* I walked to the kitchen and poured myself a glass of water, my hand shaking.

Trust him? Believe him? Believe her? Even as I considered it, I knew I had to ask Fitz and hear his side of the story. Ann and I had been enemies since she slept with my husband and conspired with him to get me fired from my job. Tommy and I were on the skids and he was hoping I'd turn to him for solace when the shit hit the fan. Instead I divorced him, and Ann lied her way out of a scandal when she claimed she was only trying to help a poor misguided student who was led astray by me.

She got a reprimand for not handling it properly, and I got fired. The student left school, Ann was eventually given a tenure-track position, and I was eventually exonerated, although I had several bad financial years until I landed at the Community College in a job I truly enjoyed.

I had no doubt Ann would do anything she could to make my life miserable, simply because I managed to land on my feet and her reputation ended up slightly tarnished. It took her years to regain her stature in the department. I, of course, never looked back.

I went back to my office to call Fitz but before I could, my doorbell rang. When I answered, I was surprised to find Mrs. Burge on my doorstep, her Cadillac Coupe de Ville parked in my drive.

"I'm sorry to stop by unannounced," the old lady said, both hands clasped atop a cane positioned in front of her. "I wanted to discuss something with you, and it seemed easier to come here than to call. May I come in?"

"Of course." I stepped to one side and she entered my foyer. "Let's go to the living room. There's a nice breeze coming in from the porch." I led the way straight ahead and gestured to the couch. "Please have a seat. Can I get you anything to drink? Some water? Lemonade?"

"I'm fine, thank you." She sat, keeping her cane near her while she shot a suspicious glance at Persuasion, who was sprawled on a chair on the porch. The cat blinked sleepily at her then settled down to snooze. Satisfied she wouldn't be bothered the old lady turned her attention to me. "I understand Samuel Collins gave you some papers that had to do with the land that is in dispute between our families."

I took a chair opposite her. "I did have some papers. I gave them to Ben Raines to evaluate. He teaches American History at Derby College."

"And they were stolen, is that correct?"

"Yes, they were. The police are working to recover them."

"Hmpf." She pursed her lips, the epitome of a disapproving old biddy from her elegantly coifed head to her dark green shoes which matched her green-flowered dress. "Did your friend have a chance to evaluate the papers before they were taken?"

I sat back, wondering where this conversation was headed. "I don't mean to sound rude, but why is that any concern of yours? Are you worried that there may be some documentation that might affect your lawsuit?"

Her hand opened and closed on the cane several times. I had the feeling she was trying to decide what to say. Finally she nodded. "You may not be aware of this, but Samuel Collins had decided to cede his rights to the land to the Sierra Club in the event of his death."

"His son mentioned something about that. I spoke with him at my party on Saturday."

"Luke." Mrs. Burge invested the word with so much disgust I'm surprised she didn't gag. "Samuel was so disappointed in his son."

"I wasn't aware of that. Mr. Collins and I weren't particularly close."

"He admired you." She said it with a mixture of disbelief and reluctance. "Your troubles with the College became known to him and he heard about what happened afterward, how you were cleared of any wrongdoing and were offered your job again but you turned it down."

I smiled briefly. "It was a token offer. If I had taken it, I'm sure I would have left by my own accord rather quickly. It's hard to work with people you can't trust."

"Indeed. I think he felt you had made the best of a bad situation and done well for yourself." It was obvious she was at least somewhat skeptical of this assertion but she was willing to pass along the information. "I'm sure that's why he decided to make you the trustee for his papers, rather than his son, who is a wastrel and a liar."

"You obviously have a very strong opinion about Luke Collins," I said, picking my words with care. "I only met him the other day and haven't had an opportunity to form any opinion about his character."

"I've known Luke Collins all his life. I've had sufficient opportunities to evaluate him." And with those words, Mrs. Burge closed that subject. "If the police recover the documents, I hope you'll verify if Samuel's will is included in them. I believe it is."

I sat up straighter in surprise. "Surely his will would be on file with his attorney, wouldn't it?"

"There is a question about his attorney and—"

My doorbell rang again, cutting off whatever she was about to say. "Excuse me," I said, getting up. "I'm not expecting anyone."

Mrs. Burge waved an imperious hand and I took that as her permission to leave. I went back to my foyer and opened the door.

Ann Burge glared at me. "What is my mother doing here?" She brushed past me and strode through the hallway to the living room.

"Come on in," I said to her back. I longed to slam the door but restrained myself.

Anne strode to Mrs. Burge. "Mother, what are you doing here?"

The old woman peered up at her daughter. "I'm chatting with a neighbor. What are you doing?" Mrs. Burge looked at me. "I didn't think you two were social friends."

"We aren't." I crossed my arms and fixed Ann with a steely glare. "Is there a reason you barged into my house?"

"I spoke with Fitz. We had lunch together." Ann returned my glare with a smirk. "He told me he read those papers you gave to Ben Raines and he didn't see anything of value."

"Jane, you said they were stolen." Mrs. Burge tapped her cane as though instructing a trained seal to answer.

"They were stolen. Copies were made, though, and

that's probably what Fitz is talking about." I forced myself to act calm and composed but inside I was seething. So not only were they having lunch, he was blabbing about the documents. That was supposed to be private information, although to be fair, perhaps we hadn't told him that. My resolve to get his side of the story started to waver.

Ann stiffened, her hands clenched at her side. "So you and he are on a first name basis now, are you? I should have known you'd do that."

"Do what?"

"Try to steal someone else's lover."

The word *lover* dropped into the room like a bomb. Mrs. Burge jerked back like she'd been hit, and I fought to remain still, freezing in place.

"Ann, quit acting like a spoiled schoolgirl," the old woman snapped. "I told you that you shouldn't run after that man."

"I did not pursue him," Ann answered haughtily, her eyes fixed on mine. "Fitz and I have an understanding." She stepped closer to me. "I don't know what kind of game you're playing but you won't win, do you hear me? You won't get him and you won't get that land for your precious turtles."

I was so angry I couldn't muster a sufficient response. Luckily, Mrs. Burge did it for me. "You're wrong, Ann. I don't know what Dr. Williams claims to have found in those documents, but it's irrelevant. Samuel Collins and I had an agreement, and I intend to uphold my end of it even if he didn't."

Ann turned slowly to stare down at her mother. "What do you mean?"

"That's why I came to see you," Mrs. Burge said to

me. "I wanted to know if Samuel's will was included in those documents he gave you."

I sank down in the chair, my legs wobbly. "I don't know," I said. "I didn't examine the files very closely."

"There wasn't any will," Ann declared. "Fitz and I discussed that. He said there were some legal papers included but he didn't mention a will. I asked him specifically."

"Why would you do that?" My head was spinning. Who to believe?

Ann blew out an impatient sigh. "Luke asked me. When he handed the papers off to you he didn't know that his father's will wasn't on file with their attorney. When he discovered that, he knew that the will might be included in those documents he gave to you."

"He should have checked that before he turned over those documents." Mrs. Burge gave a ladylike snort. "Trust Luke Collins to do something so foolish."

Ann's mouth thinned into an imperceptible line and she slowly and deliberately crossed her arms. I had the feeling she did it so she wouldn't be tempted to hit her mother. The thought surfaced then vanished quickly. "Don't let your prejudice get in the way again, Mother."

The old woman was unintimidated. She glared back at Ann defiantly. "I am more objective about this than you are, Ann. Samuel Collins and I had an agreement, and I intend to see that it is adhered to."

"What kind of agreement?" I managed to wedge in the question before Ann could open her mouth again.

"It's time for us to right an old wrong. Samuel and I discussed it and we decided that the best use for the land was to make it available to the public."

"Right what wrong?" I asked.

"It was when I was a young girl." Mrs. Burge's shoulders sagged and suddenly she didn't seem like the feisty old woman with fight still in her. Now she looked her age and more, a tired woman whose memories were weighing on her. "At the time it seemed so romantic. We even helped. Samuel and I carried notes between them. They had a special place. We called it the Mailbox Tree."

"Nobody cares about that, Mother. It happened seventy years ago. It's in the past and over."

"I care about it. Samuel cared. What does it matter how long ago it happened? It was a tragedy and one that almost repeated itself."

Ann stiffened and glared at her mother so fiercely I was sure the old woman would feel it physically. "Neither Luke nor I were that stupid," she said frostily.

"I have no idea what you're talking about," I said. "If you want to have an argument, feel free to do so but leave me out of it." I started to rise but Mrs. Burge raised a hand, and I sank back down.

"I apologize. Ann and I don't agree on this point and we never will." When Ann started to speak the old lady overrode her. "I grew up here, you see. My father was very old-fashioned. He didn't believe in allowing girls to inherit. I married a distant cousin and we kept the property in the family. I've always lived here. I know the marsh and the wildlife refuge as well as Samuel did." She glanced at Ann. "But that's not what this is about. It happened when I was a young girl. I didn't really understand what went on until I was older. No one told us about it, you see. We were children." She fell silent, staring at her hands.

"What happened?" I prompted.

"My uncle and Samuel Collins' aunt fell in love. The legal disputes about land rights had just started and tempers were running high. They decided to elope." Mrs. Burge looked to her right, at my porch, her eyes misty with memory. "Their bodies were found in the fen days later."

She fell silent, her eyes bright with tears. Ann glared at her. "It's old history, Mother."

"Did they kill themselves?" I asked gently.

The old woman turned her head slowly to meet my eyes. "That's what we were told," she said softly. "But later, Samuel found a letter from his father to my father." She stared outside again. "I think they killed them. I think our fathers did it."

Chapter 9

"Good Lord," I murmured. "How could they get away with that?"

"There is no proof," Ann snapped. "None whatsoever. Why are you bringing up this old family history? What good does that do?"

"She was pregnant, you see." Mrs. Burge focused on me again, ignoring her daughter, who stood in the middle of my living room like she owned it. "At that time, it was a horrible disgrace, not just because of the families involved but because they weren't married."

I could well imagine it. I remembered a couple of girls from my high school class who 'visited relatives' for a school year. "It must have shocked you a lot," I said. "Especially if you were a child at the time."

The old lady nodded. "Of course, nobody told us the whole story. It wasn't until Samuel and I were older that we pieced together what happened. He showed me several letters to prove what he said. I think they were in that bundle he gave to you."

"You mean the ones Luke gave to her?" Ann demanded.

Mrs. Burge regarded her daughter with imperious disdain then resumed her story. "You can imagine how upset my father was when Ann and Luke Collins started to date. That's why Luke was sent away. I suppose that's why he and his father were never close."

"You know nothing about it." Ann took a step closer to her mother and I leaned forward, ready to intervene if necessary. Ann saw my movement and shot me a venomous look but she did back off.

"I know far more than you realize. The proof is in those letters and documents Samuel gave to you." Mrs. Burge regarded me with bright, tear-filled eyes. "Samuel had the originals. He gave me copies of some of the documents, but not all. We felt it was best that we both keep a copy of the papers that have to do with the land grant and our family history because—"

"What does this have to do with the old man's will?" Ann demanded. "This is past history. Why rake it up now?"

"Samuel and I decided that it was time to put it to rest. We saw no reason to continue this feuding. He and I agreed to deed the land to the Sierra Club when we died." She frowned. "I thought he had changed his will, but apparently he hasn't." She peered up at Ann. "Or did he?"

Ann drew back. "Why are you asking me?"

"You and Luke have been spending a lot of time together. Just because he can't find the will that doesn't mean he didn't know what was in it."

"Wait a minute," I said. "What are you saying?"

The old woman tapped her cane again, obviously unhappy with her trained seal—me. "I mean that Samuel told me he discussed the change in his will with Luke. They had several heated conversations about it. And now Samuel is dead, supposedly by accident."

Ann took a step forward and this time I did spring to my feet, stepping between her and her mother. "You vengeful old woman." Ann's voice was low and hate-filled, a whisper of anger. "If you're so sure Luke had something to do with that old bastard's death, why didn't you go to the police?"

I moved to one side so Mrs. Burge could see her daughter's face. She smiled faintly. "I didn't say that Luke had anything to do with his death. After all, Luke doesn't live here. He doesn't live close to Samuel Collins. How could he have anything to do with his father's death?"

Ann's face paled so fast I was sure she might faint. "I had nothing to do with his death," she whispered. "How dare you imply that I did?"

"I think everyone needs to take a deep breath and relax," I said. "Don't say anything that you'll regret later."

"It's too late for that." Ann turned her glare on me. "I suppose you'll run to the police now and tell them what's been said."

"I don't think that's necessary," Mrs. Burge said. "The police are capable of finding the truth on their own."

"All of this is just speculation," I said. "There isn't a legal will, and as far as I know, there is no reason to believe Mr. Collins' death was anything other than an accident."

"Well, I have a legal will and it's been notarized and witnessed properly." The old lady jabbed her cane into my area rug and got laboriously to her feet. "And I have copies of correspondence between Samuel and myself in which he states his desires for the property."

"But what about the lawsuit?" I reached out to help the old lady, but she ignored me, swaying a bit when she was finally standing.

"I will testify in court that the land belongs equally to both our families. And I will testify that it should be given to the Sierra Club for their use."

"That's insane." Ann stepped back from her mother as if the older woman had an infectious disease. "That land will be worth millions once road construction is underway."

"What?" This was news to me. I knew the land in question was worth some money, but millions? "How can that be?"

"Subdivisions and strip malls." Mrs. Burge walked slowly toward the front door and I fell into step with her. Ann trailed behind us. "We made a million dollars on this subdivision and that was decades ago. The land will be sold in parcels to developers. Commercial developers will pay a pretty penny to have land for restaurants, gas stations, and shopping malls." Her lips thinned in disgust. "Samuel was right. Someone needs to make restitution for the anguish this land has caused."

"You can't do this. It's not just our family who might profit," Ann said. "Several other people and groups have bought land."

"The college," I said, remembering Mr. Collins' letter. "And Fitz Williams."

"Among others." Ann brushed past her mother to reach the door ahead of us. "What happens to them if you relinquish the land where the fen is?"

"Their property is useless unless the road goes in," Mrs. Burge said. "As you well know. And as they well knew when they purchased it."

"Useless?" I asked.

"Unless someone wants to build a home next to a

marsh." Mrs. Burge shook her head. "Those people bought land with the hope they could sell it again and make a profit. I have no sympathy for them if they're stuck with what they bought."

I had never asked Fitz about the land. Was she right? Was he only in it for profit? He said something about building a home there, but could I believe him about that? Not all the land needed for the construction was near the marsh. Maybe he bought something further south, away from the fen.

"You can't just give up the lawsuit," Ann argued. "The people who bought land will sue us. They had an expectation that the construction would go through. If you try to give the land away now, it will tie up the project for years."

"It still might go through," I pointed out. "The government has been known to seize land and push through their projects regardless of who it harms."

"I don't care," Mrs. Burge said clearly. "For once in my life I will do what I feel is the right thing to do instead of the thing that benefits me the most. They can fight about it when I'm gone. I will make sure my wishes are known."

"You're deluding yourself if you think you can make that happen." Ann jerked open my front door. "The only creatures that construction could harm are a bunch of stupid turtles and a few butterflies. Nobody cares about that." She stalked down my sidewalk, got into her sports car, and sped off without a backward glance.

"I'm sorry you had to be party to our disagreement," Mrs. Burge said, watching the red car disappear from sight. She sighed and began walking, and I went with her. She seemed more tottery than before, less strong. I think the argument had sapped her strength, if not her physical strength, then her emotional strength.

"I'm confused," I admitted. "It doesn't matter what was in Mr. Collins' will. And I'm sorry, but it doesn't matter what's in your will. Unless his will is found, and unless you—" I stopped, realizing what I was about to say.

"Unless I die?" She opened her dark green handbag and found her car keys. "I received some interesting legal advice recently that has led me to believe that is not the case. Apparently I have options in that regard."

"What do you mean?"

She opened her driver's door. "I can cede the land to the Sierra Club now with the proviso that it be given to them permanently when I die. Once we find Samuel's will, it can address any other lingering issues."

"But what if his will can't be found?"

She smiled faintly. "I'm sure it will be. You see, I know where a copy is. He and I made sure to keep notarized copies of both of our wills to be sure they were safe. It was sentimental, perhaps, and childish, but it made us feel better. I'll see to it that his will is read in court. Samuel made sure a legal copy was on file with his lawyer, but another copy was kept safe and sound because..." Her eyes grew cold, any trace of sentimentality gone. "He didn't trust his lawyer, so he made sure other copies were kept." She nodded, white hair wisping in the breeze. "Yes, it's very appropriate that the true copy be kept there."

"Where?"

"I may need help retrieving it," she said. "If I do, I'll call on you."

"I don't understand." I helped her into her car, holding onto her arm as she slid into the driver's seat. "What do you need help with?"

"Don't worry about it." She smiled up at me and this time it seemed genuine. It was as if a burden was lifted and she was able to finally relax. "Ann may think she'll get what she wants, but it won't work out the way she thinks it will."

"What does she want?" I asked when Mrs. Burge started the car.

She either didn't hear me or didn't care to answer. I stepped back when the car began backing down my drive. The old woman drove away with an expression of single-minded determination on her lined face.

I went back slowly into the house, mulling over everything. Phrases buzzed in my brain. The 'interesting legal advice' had to be from Fitz. It was one of the things he and George argued about.

I stopped in my tracks. Good Lord, I never even questioned Fitz about that. Somehow that whole brouhaha with George had completely fled my mind. Of course, I was worried about Ben, and wondering about Fitz, and trying to write a novel, and teach classes, and—

I shook my head and went back into the house. It was time to get my life back on track. The last few days had been a crazy merry-go-round with stops at random places. It was time to go straight ahead instead of circles, and the first place to start was with Fitz Williams.

I changed clothes into lightweight jeans and a loose

cotton top then I went to my office to shut down my computer. As I did, I noticed the pages from days ago when Ben handed them to me at the town meeting. It felt like centuries had passed. Was it only a week? Last Thursday was the meeting when I saw Fitz for the first time.

I stuffed the pages back into my book bag with my other SOFT information, including Mr. Collins' letter. I took the bag and my purse and left the house, compiling a list of questions in my mind while I drove to Manortown.

When I got to Fitz's house, I parked in the driveway and took a moment to compose my thoughts. He stepped onto the front step, smiling. My heart did an odd little two-step at the sight of him. He wore black jeans and a light brown shirt that highlighted his dark brown eyes. He met me as I walked to the house.

"I thought we could eat in back, on the patio," he said. "It's such a beautiful night." He noticed the book bag slung over my shoulder and asked with a laugh in his voice, "Did you bring homework to do?"

"I had an odd day today," I said. "I thought maybe you could help me make sense of it."

"I'm flattered you think I can. I'll try to live up to your expectations. Come inside and we'll get a drink then go outside and sit." He led the way into the house and gave me a tour of the small bungalow. As I suspected, it was charming with polished woodwork, Craftsman details throughout, and several leaded windows that were beautiful.

"It's a lovely home," I finally said when we were in the kitchen and he was pouring two glasses of wine. A delicious aroma emanated from the stove, and a small table was set with china and silverware.

"I was lucky to get it. The couple who lived here was very fussy about who they wanted in the house. They didn't put it on the market, but had their realtor screen house hunters to see if one popped up that would suit them. As it turns out, I did." He handed me a glass of white wine. "Let's sit outside. I went to the Farmer's Market today and decided to make vegetarian lasagna," he said. "The produce was so enticing. It's in the oven staying warm so we can eat anytime."

Fitz opened the French doors leading to a small brick patio that had just enough room for four chairs under an awning with two end tables between them. The patio was above the garden, set below us down a small slope. "Did you talk to Ben today?" he asked.

I took a seat and set my bags next to me on the ground. "Yes, I did. He sounded like he was on the mend."

Fitz grinned. "I think Charlotte has a lot to do with that. They're like besotted teenagers. Not that I'm mocking her. Charlotte deserves happiness in her life and if Ben can provide it, I'm happy."

"I feel the same about him. When I was married he was a tried and true friend." I sipped my wine then smiled ruefully. "He recognized my ex-husband's true nature. He knew better than I did what an idiot Tommy was."

"From what Ben told me, Ann had something to do with your breakup." Fitz kept his voice light.

"I never really had any proof of that," I admitted. "I think she and Tommy were having an affair, but really, it was just the icing on the cake. Tommy was a philanderer from the start. I suspect he had other girls on the side, too. That's the problem with marrying somebody who's handsome and charming. So often they don't have the character to match their appearance."

"I suppose that's true of women, too. So often a beautiful woman can prove to be less than beautiful in character." Fitz shot me a bemused look. "This is an odd conversation to be having. As I recall, we were talking about Ben, weren't we?"

"Yes, we were. I'm so glad he's making a speedy recovery." I decided it was time to pry a bit and perhaps find the answer to one of my questions. "Ben said you were going through those files you got from his backup drive."

Fitz nodded. "I did skim most of them. I practiced contract law for years. I'd need to check details, but some of those documents, if filed correctly, may shed some light on the ownership question of the land for the construction project."

"I'm curious about that." I seized the opening he gave me. "Why did you buy the land in the construction zone?"

"Didn't we talk about that?" He looked at me, puzzled. "I hoped to build a home there. I didn't know how close the government was to funding that project."

"Did you know how valuable the land might be if the project went through?" I tried to sound merely curious and not accusatory, but I'm not sure I succeeded.

"I found out after I purchased it. Why do you ask?"

"I just wondered, that's all. I guess it's part of my odd day."

"That's right. You mentioned that. Tell me about

it."

"I'm not sure where to start," I said, struggling to remember the questions I had formulated during my drive. Fitz's laid-back manner made it hard to think of him as a philanderer or a thief.

"Why don't you start with what's bothering you the most?" He sipped his wine and set the glass on the glass-topped wicker table between us. "You're obviously distracted."

"I am?"

Fitz nodded, the picture of the relaxed host. "You barely said a word when I showed you around the house and you haven't expressed a single opinion about anything." He smiled, his dimples making an appearance. "That isn't like you, Jane."

I was tongue-tied. I hid it by opening my bag and pulling out the letter Mr. Collins gave me. I handed it to Fitz. "Are you the person he means in this letter? Are you the one who gave him legal advice? Him and Mrs. Burge?"

He stared at the letter, frowning. "I've seen penmanship like this before," he murmured. "Some of those files Ben had were like this. I wasn't sure who the author was, but, yes, it makes sense that it might be Samuel Collins, I suppose."

"You see what he says there, about the unsavory practices on the part of the college." I pointed to the middle of the note.

"And the landowners." Fitz folded the note and handed it back to me. "Do you think I'm involved in unsavory practices?" He kept his tone light but I heard the underlying annoyance in his voice.

"I don't know what to think," I said bluntly. "Mr.

Collins left that note in my mailbox on the day he died. He left that and a bunch of other documents." I fumbled in my book bag. "Do you recognize this information? Was it in those files that Ben scanned?"

Fitz took the clipped set of chronological notes and skimmed through them. "This is one of the documents I noted to be of interest. The original of this was handwritten. I suggested to Ben that he check to see the filing date for some of these sales." He handed the pages back to me.

I glanced at the list of dates, names, and notes. That's what was wrong with the information. In several spots a name was listed along with 'date of sale' and 'date of deed transfer' but in a couple of other spots there was no 'date of deed transfer.' "Don't land transactions have to have a deed attached?"

"Not all, but most have some ancillary information about the land history, previous ownership, specifications about property size and its location, and so on." He sipped his wine, watching me put the papers back into my bag. "So Mr. Collins himself gave you more documents in addition to the ones his son gave you after his father died?"

"Yes. I gave them to Ben. Ann was there when I did." I watched Fitz, waiting to see what his reaction would be. "I don't think anyone else knew that Ben had those documents."

Fitz nodded thoughtfully. "I doubt if Ann attacked Ben," he said. "Is that what you're getting at?"

"I'm not getting at anything." I couldn't think of a good way to work the conversation around to the missing files, not to mention his continuing relationship with Ann. "I'm just confused, that's all. Ann and Mrs.

Burge came to my house today and had one heck of an argument. A lot of things were said that just added to my confusion."

"About what?"

I abandoned any pretense of tact. "Part of it was about you."

His face stilled and wary curiosity replaced his earlier easy-going expression. "What about me? I barely know Mrs. Burge. Why would they argue about me?"

"Ann said you and she were lovers. Ben said he called your office today and Ann was there. He said it sounded—" I fumbled for words. "It sounded like he was interrupting something. Ben said she answered the phone."

"I left the office briefly to speak with a student in the hallway. Perhaps he called then. She and I were arguing and I didn't want the student to overhear."

"Oh." It certainly sounded plausible enough. And Ann was certainly devious enough to pretend nothing was wrong just for the sake of putting on a good front. "I suppose Ben might have been mistaken."

"It appears that you prefer to believe rumor rather than me," Fitz said in a low voice. "I told you there is nothing between Ann and I and I meant it. I'm not sure what else you need to know about my relationship with her."

"Ann tells a different story," I said stubbornly, remembering the smirky way Ann acted when she talked about Fitz earlier at my house.

"Ann is lying. I'm sure she's doing it to drive a wedge between us. I've come to believe that's the sort of thing she'd do. And it appears that she's succeeding." Fitz stared at me, his body stiff and unyielding. Gone was the genial, relaxed host. I could see the lawyer in the way he examined me, evaluated me, and judged me. "What else do you have to ask me?"

"I'm sorry if I've hurt your feelings," I said. "It's just that Ann said point-blank that you and she have an understanding."

"Let me make this very clear. She and I have never slept together. I have no desire to sleep with her. It's been convenient for her and I to attend various social events together, but that is the extent of our relationship. I think Ann feels exactly the same way because I know she already has a significant relationship in her life." Fitz swallowed more wine, but his movements were jerky and he spilled some wine on the table. He ignored it and stared at me as though challenging him.

"What do you mean?"

"I mean that Ann often goes away for the weekend and I suspect it's because she's visiting someone. I assumed it was a lover, or someone else she's close to." He drummed his fingers on the arm of his chair. "Did anything else arise from this discussion with Ann and her mother, anything else you care to accuse me about?"

"I'm not accusing," I said quickly. "Like I said, I'm just confused. Mrs. Burge said that she sought legal advice, and in his letter, Mr. Collins said he did, too. Are you the person they asked?"

"Why do you want to know?"

"You don't have an unbiased opinion in all of this," I said.

"All of what?"

"The land, the construction project, those files of Ben's. If the construction goes through, you'll make a lot of money. But Mrs. Burge told me she had decided to give the land away. Your claim to the land would be in jeopardy and you might lose money. Did she know that when she asked for your advice? Did she know that you had bought land?"

He was silent for a long moment then he said, "It's a good thing you are simply being blunt. Otherwise I'd think you're trying to insult me."

I felt my own temper start to fray. He was acting overbearing again, something that always put me on edge. "I also had a question about those files of Ben's."

"What about them? I reviewed them and I gave him my legal opinion."

"Did he talk to you about them?"

"I just told you. I gave him some legal advice."

"No, did you talk to him about the files? He compared what's on the backup drive to what's in the online backups. He thought perhaps some were missing."

Fitz stared at me, his eyes cold. "I beg your pardon?"

"Ben said that the scans were numbered, but when he checked the files in the online backup drive, there were differences between the online files and the ones on the backup drive. He said that it appeared many files were missing."

"And you think I deleted them. Why would I do that? I'm sure you have a theory." His cold eyes accented his acid tone of voice.

"I—I'm not—that is, I don't know." I stammered,

surprised by the cold anger that radiated from him.

"You're not sure? Isn't that what you were going to say?"

I stared him down. "Yes, I have a theory. Perhaps those papers would benefit the construction project or hinder it in some way. Perhaps you saw them and realized if you deleted them, it might help you when it came time to sell the land."

"And I suppose you'll accuse me next of giving Mrs. Burge and Mr. Collins bad advice in order to further my own monetary gains."

When he said it that way, it sounded so awful. Surely he wouldn't do something so despicable, would he? "I don't think so, no. But what am I supposed to believe?" I asked, tossing my hands up. "I just met you a week ago and I barely know you. I've known Ben all my life and I trust him when he says something was altered. I've known Mrs. Burge for years and she has no reason to lie to me, either."

"But I do, is that right? Is that what you're saying? What do you think my motive is?"

"I don't know. I have no idea. Maybe you and Ann are working together to make a killing when you sell the land. Maybe you're trying to protect the college. Maybe you just made a mistake and bought land without knowing its history."

"I think I did make a mistake. The mistake was to trust you."

I glared at him. "I've been honest with you. Ben expressed his concerns and I asked you about it."

"You implied I removed valuable information in order to profit from it." Fitz stood. "I think it's time you left."

I put the note into my bag and stood slowly. "Will you answer one more question for me?" I asked.

He nodded once, brusquely.

"Did you and George Wick get into a fight on Sunday?"

Fitz studied me for a moment then he nodded again. "It wasn't much of a fight, but yes, I did hit him."

"Why?"

"That doesn't concern you." He shifted his gaze to his garden. "Given the circumstances, I think you should tell Mrs. Knight that I won't be participating in her garden event this year."

I stepped in front of him, forcing him to see me. "Tell me."

He gave me a look of such disdain I immediately stepped back. He stepped onto the stone walkway, and I belatedly saw that he was leading me back to my car. I grabbed my bag and purse, then followed him.

"There were two reasons," he said. "George made a rude remark about you. At the time, I didn't know you well, but I refuse to hear anyone demeaned in such a manner." He fell silent.

"What was the second reason?"

His lips thinned and I thought he'd refuse to answer. We passed through the wisteria-laden arbor and entered the front yard. "I did give legal advice to Mr. Collins and Mrs. Burge. George Wick and his father before him had provided legal services to both families. Based on the questions they asked me, I came to the conclusion that George had, at best, given them incorrect advice and at worst, he had defrauded them."

His face was harsh. "I know you won't believe this

of me, but that angered me a great deal. They are elderly people and as such, they are often vulnerable to others who would prey on them. I decided to let George know exactly how I felt."

"Thank you." I brushed past him and went to my car.

He took a few steps after me. "For what?"

I opened my door and tossed my bags inside. "I don't know what to believe in regard to those missing files. But I do believe you about Ann. And I believe that you acted honorably when it came to Mrs. Burge and Mr. Collins. So I guess, well, thank you for not totally being an asshole." I smiled tentatively.

"I'm sorry you couldn't trust me." His voice was level, but his eyes held accusation.

I thought carefully about what to say. "I've known Ben for a long time. I asked him to talk to you about those files, and he said he would. Once I hear from him, I'll know if I can trust you or not."

Fitz shook his head slowly. "Trust doesn't work that way, Jane."

I had no answer for that. I got into my car and drove away, tears trailing down my cheeks. I had handled it badly and in doing so I lost his respect and his trust. The only way I could come out a winner in this situation was if he proved to be a liar and a thief because that would mean my accusations were true.

Somehow I just didn't believe that of him. Fitz Williams might be over-confident and arrogant, but I didn't really believe that he bought that land in order to make money on it. But how to explain the missing files? Fitz was the only person who handled that backup drive. If he inadvertently deleted something, surely he would know it.

I got home and immediately changed into my gardening clothes. I always found solace in physical activity, and I tackled my back yard, weeding, mowing, transplanting, and trimming until sweat ran down my face, mingling with the tear tracks. I replayed the conversation over and over in my mind and came up with a dozen other things to say, none of which made any sense now, of course.

I took a short break and sharpened the claws on my hoe-fork combo tool and the edge on my handheld weeder. Then I moved to the front yard and worked until full dark, only stopping when it was difficult to see where I was going.

I left my tools in my sand bucket by the garage because I was too exhausted to clean them properly. I went inside and peeled off my clothes, dropping them by the bed. I showered and dressed in my sleep T-shirt then self-medicated with two glasses of wine and an over-the-counter sleep aid. I did not want to continue replaying that night's fiasco in my mind.

I fell into bed and didn't wake up until I heard a voice or voices outside. I struggled to sit up, but the combination of wine and medication kept me pinned to the bed. I fell back asleep and didn't wake up fully until I heard shouting.

Chapter 10

I sprang from bed and dragged on the first clothes that came to hand—the dirty gardening clothes from the night before. I raced out of my bedroom then I stopped.

What time was it? Who was shouting? The houses in their neighborhood were set so far apart that it had to be extremely loud shouting for me to hear it. I went into the kitchen and peered at the digital numbers on the stove display. Five-thirty. The light outside, soft through the trees in the back yard, told me it was morning, not night.

Who was shouting at five-thirty in the morning?

I slipped into my garden clogs and took my house keys from the dish in my office before going through the front door. I headed left where Rosings Drive wended down a slight hill to the other houses. That's when I saw the Burge house, across the street and at the bottom of the road. Smoke billowed up from the roof and the upper windows. Flames were shooting up from the roof and the attached garage. Someone was in front of the house, shouting.

I ran back inside my house and dialed 911. "There's a fire, west of town. The Rosings subdivision." I gave hurried directions then hung up and ran down the street.

Ann Burge stood outside the house dressed in a silky housecoat that left little to the imagination. It outlined every contour and curve of her body. "What happened?" I demanded, skidding to a stop in front of her.

"I don't know. I saw the flames from my house. Something woke me and—Luke! Mother is inside, I'm sure of it!" She turned to Luke Collins, who burst from the Collins house across the street. "I'm sure she's still in there. I don't know what happened. I was asleep and a noise woke me and—"

Collins took her by the arms and gave her a little shake. He was dressed in a white T-shirt and jeans with unlaced sneakers. If he noticed Ann's dishabille, he didn't show it. "Where does she sleep? Does she still sleep upstairs?"

Ann shook her head, dark red hair flying around her face in disarray. "She sleeps in the old study, downstairs. In the back."

He released her and she stumbled back. He ran to the house and up the front sidewalk. I started to follow but Ann caught my arm. "You can't go in there!" she shouted. "It's too dangerous!"

I glanced down at her feet. She wore stylish slippers, more of a sandal with open toes and tops. "He might need help." I shook her off and followed Luke, running as fast as I could up the front steps. I tried hard not to see around me, not to smell smoke or feel heat when I burst through the front door after him.

Smoke billowed above me. When I took a breath, it felt hot and I choked, gagging so badly I had to reel back onto the porch to suck in some oxygen. It took a second or two, but I finally managed to get enough air in that I could go back inside.

Noise enveloped me. Roaring, groaning, creaking,

popping—it surrounded me on all sides, like some kind of crazy orchestral warm-up screaming at high volume. It wasn't just the noise. The smoke was so thick I could barely tell I was in a house. I might have been walking through a forest or a shopping mall. The heat was intense and also enveloping, like I'd walked into an electric blanket that touched me here and there, no one spot too hot to hurt but overall making me feel sunburnt.

I entered a large open foyer with an arched doorway on my left, a staircase on my right and another arched doorway straight ahead. The whole space was soft white once, but now it was gray with ashes and smoke and debris billowing about. I spied a long hall through the archway in front of me and thought I glimpsed movement there. I started forward but heat from my left made me hesitate. The room was filled with smoke and flames that poked and danced throughout the room, mainly on the outside wall on the far side of the room. A large couch was on fire, and as I watched, it seemed to melt, fabric oozing away while flames consumed it.

I pulled my T-shirt up over my mouth and breathed shallowly through my nose, struggling for air. I could barely see through the smoke and my tears. Heat and dust blew into my face, adding to my misery. I stumbled forward, tripping on a rug and banging into a large round table. The tall vase in the center of the table toppled and rolled off, exploding into pieces on the slippery tiled floor.

The smoke was a blanket, a heavy, acrid blanket that suffocated me while it twined around me. I moved forward, waving away thick streamers of gray until I could see the doorway once again. I went into the hall and the smoke was lighter here, the heat and the flames and the noise diminished.

"Luke!" I screamed. "Mrs. Burge! Catherine!" I doubt anyone could hear me. The noise from the flames was all-encompassing. A closed door on my left felt hot to the touch. If it was closed, Luke probably hadn't gone that way. That was my chaotic reasoning, at least. I continued but the smoke was so thick I didn't see the body until I fell over it.

I landed on my side, my face slamming into a doorframe. For an instant I was dazed, blackness blotting out everything around me. Then I gasped in a lungful of smoke and began to choke, pushing up onto my hands and knees and letting my head hang down while I struggled to get air. Bile rushed up and I choked on it, too, until I finally got my panic under control.

I felt around on the floor near me and touched someone's arm. I latched on and began dragging the person back the way I'd come, scooting on my butt with painful digs of my feet into the carpeted hallway. At some point I dragged myself upright and reached down, finding two hands. I latched onto the wrists and began pulling the dead weight back down the hall, walking backwards and praying nothing behind me would trip me.

I wasn't even sweating. I think the sweat evaporated because I was so hot. I don't know how long I dragged and pulled and cried, but suddenly someone was there, wrapping arms around me and tugging me back. I lost my grip on the wrists and kicked feebly to get loose, to get back to saving whoever it was who was lying in that hall.

The person holding me wrapped his arms around me and manhandled me from the house. I think I passed out briefly because I choked so badly, gasping and retching on smoke and fear. Then I was lying on the grass of the lawn. I turned my head and saw a fireman running into the house, a long hose trailing behind him.

A paramedic leaned over me. "Let's get you away from here," he said, gesturing to someone else. I was moved onto a stretcher and taken into the street where the ambulance was parked. I glimpsed people carrying someone else on another stretcher, someone in jeans and a burned T-shirt. Ann was bending over him, holding his hand and weeping while the paramedics moved him to another ambulance.

They must have given me something for the pain because the next thing I knew, I was moving, or rather, the ambulance I was in was moving. I was faintly aware of the wailing of the siren but it seemed far away.

"Am I deaf?" I whispered.

A man was near me, sitting on a bench or seat of some kind. I don't think he heard me.

"Am I deaf?" I said, louder. That hurt so bad I started to choke.

The man leaned over me. "Don't talk. Your throat is hurt."

Hurt? What did that mean? I tried to speak, but he shook his head and leaned over me, pressing a button on a panel on my left side.

I woke up in the hospital. Ben and Charlotte stood at the foot of my bed, looking anxious. "Hey," I whispered. "What's going on? What day is it?"

"Still Thursday," Ben said, glancing quickly to his left. "It's Thursday afternoon. The fire was early this morning. You got singed, but your burns aren't too bad. But your hair is kinda goofy."

I touched my head with partially bandaged hands. My palms itched like crazy and were hot, but my fingers appeared to be fine. I winced when I felt that some of my hair had burned away. I felt big chunks gone and frazzled ends for other bits. "Guess I'll need a new hairstyle," I whispered, my throat raw and burning. "Is Luke okay? Was that him I rescued?"

Ben nodded. "He's got some burns, too, but he'll be okay."

Charlotte started to speak, but a man in a suit came into view, walking around the privacy curtain that blocked my view of the rest of the room. He was a lumpy person with a bland, unremarkable face except for small, sharp dark eyes that seemed to flit here and there. "Miss Austin, I'm Detective Forster. I have a few questions if you feel up to answering them." He moved aside his suit coat so I could see a badge clipped to his belt.

I ignored him and turned my attention to Charlotte and Ben. "What's happened?"

Charlotte came around the bed to sit cautiously next to me on my left. "Mrs. Burge is dead." She glanced at the officer, who stood on my right side. "She was murdered."

"Holy buckets," I coughed.

"With your garden weeder," Ben said.

It wasn't a bad dream. The firemen found Mrs. Burge's body, burned but recognizable, with my garden tool stabbed through her heart. There was no doubt it was mine. I used an ergonomic variety with a padded handle, part of a matching set of tools.

How did they know it was mine? Apparently Ann remembered it from the party when she and Fitz were there. She identified it.

I added that to my growing list of grievances against Ann Burge.

The detective shooed Ben and Charlotte from my room and proceeded to interrogate me. I considered calling for a lawyer, but the only two lawyers I knew—George Wick and Fitz Williams—both hated my guts. I figured I was better off without them.

"I have no idea how my garden tool got there," I said for the third time. "The last time I saw it, I put it in my bucket on Wednesday evening. I always do that after I work with tools to keep them from rusting."

"Can anyone else corroborate that?"

"No, because I was alone," I repeated, again for the third time.

"I've been told you and Mrs. Burge argued earlier in the day yesterday."

"We did not," I managed to state around my open-mouthed astonishment. "Mrs. Burge and her daughter argued in my presence. I did not argue with anyone."

"I see." He jotted a note in a spiral notepad and regarded me with the same bland curiosity he'd exhibited during the entire twenty minutes of speaking with me. "What did they argue about?"

"They argued about me." Fitz walked into the room carrying a leather briefcase, all very businesslike in a three-piece suit, striped tie, and shiny Oxford shoes. "I'm Miss Austin's lawyer. If you have any further questions for her, you can ask them while I am present."

My first feeling was one of relief. Then I

remembered I looked like death warmed over, my hair was in ragged clumps, Fitz was pissed off at me, and did I really trust him?

Did I have a choice? I smiled at him but he didn't even glance at me. He kept his attention fixed on the detective. Fitz was so handsome in his dark suit, his curly hair tamed into submission with just a hint of rambunctiousness at the back. A good suit is like a uniform, it transforms any man but it really did something for Fitz. It made me realize how sophisticated, how old-school, upper-class-rich he really was.

"Perhaps Miss Austin can tell me about the argument she overheard," the detective said, emphasis on *overheard*.

I reached for the water glass on the tray in front of me. My throat hurt so bad but I was damned if I'd use that as an excuse. Fitz noticed and handed me the glass, which I fumbled because of my bandages. He held it steady for me and I sipped, acutely aware of my shabby hospital gown and ratty hair.

I leaned back and whispered, "Mrs. Burge told me that she knew for certain Mr. Collins would leave the land to the Sierra Club." The detective frowned at me, and I added, "The land where a big construction project is slated to go through."

"How did she know that?" he asked, jotting a note.

"Apparently she made the same stipulation in her will." I glanced at Fitz for confirmation, but he kept his attention on the detective, who was busily jotting something in his notepad.

"Why did that cause an argument?" Detective Forster asked, his head still lowered. "Did you object to that plan?"

"I didn't argue with her," I said before Fitz could speak. "Her daughter, Ann, argued with her."

"Why were they arguing at your house?"

I raised my arms and slapped them on the bed. "Ow!"

Fitz turned. "What's wrong?"

I raised my right arm so he could see the bandage that covered my palm and most of my forearm. "I forgot I was burned. Damn it."

His mouth tensed into a thin line, an expression I was starting to recognize as Fitz Is Pissed. He turned back to the detective. "My client is injured and needs time to rest. Do you have any other questions?"

"As a matter of fact, I do." The detective regarded me. "Did Mrs. Burge have any proof that Mr. Collins planned to change his will?"

"I'm not sure. I think she had a copy of his will. She said something like that." I tried to remember the conversation from yesterday, but today's events kept intruding. "She said something about correspondence or something. And she did say she had made her wishes known."

"Her wish that this land under contention be given to the Sierra Club?" Forster asked.

I nodded and reached for the water again. I managed it myself this time, but Fitz watched, I suppose thinking I might douse myself if I wasn't careful. I couldn't interpret his expression. On the one hand, I think he was concerned, but maybe he was just angry. Probably at me for interrupting his day off. Why the hell was he here? I didn't call him, and he certainly wasn't my attorney of record. I didn't have an attorney of record. I made a mental note to rectify that as soon as I could. An attorney might be useful to have around.

"You belong to a group that is trying to stop this construction project from going through, don't you?"

I put the now empty water glass back on the tray. "I do. I'm on the committee along with several other concerned citizens."

"So if the land is given to the Sierra Club, that benefits you."

"It benefits the group to which she belongs," Fitz corrected. "It will not benefit her personally."

"Really? Doesn't she live near the construction site? I was under the impression the neighborhood where the fire occurred and where Miss Austin lives is near the impending road work." The detective's incurious gaze settled on me.

"It is also near Miss Burge, the Collins home, and other homes in the area. It is not solely Miss Austin's neighborhood." Fitz's tone of voice was neutral but firm.

Forster nodded. "Indeed. Tell me, Miss Austin. Can you think of any reason someone would want to kill Mrs. Catherine Burge?"

"I don't think it's necessary for my client to answer that. Anything she might say would be an opinion, and as such it's irrelevant in a court of law." Fitz moved so he blocked the detective from getting any closer to me. "As I said, Miss Austin has been injured and needs to rest. Perhaps your questions can wait until she's released from the hospital."

"Mr. Luke Collins has a copy of his father's will and it does not mention anything about the Sierra Club. The property is left to Luke Collins."

"Then it's not the most current will," I said.

"Really? Are you so sure? It was dated ten years ago and prepared by Mr. Collins' lawyer." The detective glanced at Fitz. "Mr. George Wick."

If George was involved, fraud was surely involved, too. "I was told another will was made more recently than that."

"Did Mrs. Burge tell you that she had changed her will so if she died the land would go to the Sierra Club?" Forster persisted.

I nodded. "I think she did."

"So your group would benefit if she died."

"I must insist that you leave now." Fitz stepped directly in front of Forster. "Miss Austin is exhausted and needs her rest."

The man returned Fitz's gaze with an equally assessing one. "Do you mind telling me why they argued about you?"

"That isn't relevant to your investigation," Fitz answered promptly.

"I'll decide what's relevant," the detective snapped.

"Do you have a signed statement by Miss Ann Burge about the conversation?" Fitz turned to his briefcase, which he had set on the visitor chair next to my bed. He clicked it open and extracted a piece of paper.

"I have her statement but I haven't had a formal interview with her yet," Detective Forster said.

"I see." Fitz held up the paper. "This is a request for a subpoena which I intend to serve on Miss Ann Burge requiring her to testify truthfully regarding her conversation with Miss Austin on Wednesday, June

17th in the afternoon at Miss Austin's residence." He
turned back to the briefcase and found another paper. "I
am also planning to subpoena several witnesses as to
the location of Miss Austin's garden tools and have
them state their knowledge of where her tools were
kept, and that others had knowledge of that location."
He laid the papers on the bed near me. "Shall I
continue? I have several other court papers prepared."

The detective slowly closed his little notepad and
tucked it into his suit pocket. I had to admit, his suit
suffered by comparison to Fitz's, which was crisply
pressed and beautifully tailored. I could so easily
imagine the body underneath Fitz's suit, and the
thought of it made me warmer than I already was from
my burns.

"We'll continue our discussion when you're
feeling more recovered, Miss Austin." The detective
nodded to me, a ponderous dipping of his balding head.

"Only if I am present," Fitz said. "Thank you." He
turned his back on the detective and faced me.

I peered up seeking—what? Reassurance? Hope? I
don't know what I wanted to see but what I saw was a
cool, assessing expression, which was better than the
Fitz Pissed one. I peeked past him and saw the detective
leaving the room. "Thank you," I whispered.

His expression seemed to thaw for an instant. He
touched my bandaged hand gently then he stepped
back. "Ben asked me to help." He swept the papers into
his briefcase and closed it with sharp clicks of the
locks. "You need to talk to him about those files." He
was gone before I could decide what to say.

As soon as Fitz left, Charlotte came in the room.
"Just the woman I want to see," I said, pushing at the

covers draped over me. "I need to use the bathroom. Help me up."

"I don't think you're supposed to be up and walking around," she said doubtfully.

"I don't have anything stuck in me." I raised my arms so she could see. "If I'm not hooked up, I'm mobile, or so I say. Come on. Help me."

She lent me an arm and helped me totter to the room's bathroom, a tiny room next to the door. I managed to do my business without embarrassing myself and finally regarded myself in the mirror.

Holy buckets, I was a fright. My hair was burned off on the left side of my head. My skin was red, my eyes were red, and I had an enormous purpling bruise on my right temple. "I'm surprised Fitz didn't run screaming out of the room when he saw me," I said to Charlotte while she helped me back to the bed.

"He had other things to worry about. Ben called him as soon as we found out that Mrs. Burge was killed with your garden thingie."

"A weeder," I said, crawling back into the bed. "It's a digger. I always keep mine sharp so I can nip off the weeds. Who would kill her? And why?"

"Ann," Charlotte said. "Don't they always suspect the heir?"

"But according to Mrs. Burge, Ann wasn't her heir. Mrs. Burge had changed her will."

"That doesn't matter if it isn't on file, though. Did she make sure a copy was filed with her attorney?"

"George Wick is her attorney. God knows what's on file with him, that sneaky son of a bitch." I dragged the covers over me. "How long do I have to stay here? Did you talk to the doctor? I can leave soon, can't I?"

"I'm not sure. I think they were worried about a concussion since you have that nasty bruise on your face." Charlotte regarded me sympathetically. "Mr. Collins' funeral is tomorrow. I read about it in the newspaper."

I ran a hand over my clumpy hair. "I have to go. Do you think I can get a haircut before then? My regular person is on vacation." Then I heard what I was saying. "Crap, a haircut is the least of my worries. I might get thrown in jail if I'm not careful."

"Fitz won't let that happen." Ben walked into the room. "I just talked to him. He said the detective was just fishing for information. They have no proof that you did anything. The fact that your tools were kept outside means anyone could get them. Did you hear anything unusual last night?"

I started to shake my head then I slowly nodded. "I think something did wake me up but I'm not sure. I was so upset last night I took two sleeping pills washed down with a glass of wine and fell asleep right away."

"Upset about what?" Charlotte slipped her arm through Ben's and leaned against him.

"Fitz and I had an argument," I admitted. "That's why I was surprised to see him here."

Ben smiled ruefully. "He told me that you mentioned the mix-up with the files."

"Mix-up?" My attention zeroed in on him. "What mix-up?"

"I called the online backup people about it. I wasn't sure exactly how that worked." He smiled at Charlotte and she smiled in return.

"And?" I prompted when he seemed disinclined to continue.

"Oh, yeah. The files. What happens is the online backup program doesn't make backups in sequence. It sort of goes around and checks for any files that are new or changed and backs them up first. Then it goes back and compares files it already backed up and if they changed, it backs them up."

"So what does that have to do with the backup disk that Fitz was using?"

"Nothing, really. I was just trying to explain why some of the files got backed up and some didn't. What Fitz did with the backup disk was he started sorting the files. He created some directories and sub-directories and moved files around. I guess he was trying to put them into some kind of sequential order, which really had nothing to do with the order that I scanned them."

I stared at him. "You're saying that there aren't any missing files? Yesterday you were sure Fitz might have deleted something."

Ben shrugged. "I was wrong. And that's not the only thing I was wrong about." His fair skin flushed. "There's nothing going on between Fitz and Ann Burge. I misunderstood what I heard. Ann was just acting like, well, like Ann."

I fell back on the bed, limp with disbelief. "I can't believe it. You were so certain yesterday that Fitz was acting badly, and here you're saying there's no problem at all." Charlotte started to speak but stopped. I glared at her. "Go ahead. Say it."

"It's just that, well, it seems like you're always ready to believe the worst when it comes to Fitz," she said cautiously. "I don't think anyone else would have jumped to those conclusions."

"Ben did," I pointed out. "And he told me."

"I didn't say he manipulated the files." Ben sounded defensive, probably because he knew he'd goofed up, big-time. "I said it might be possible. You were the one who assumed he did something wrong."

I began to argue but stopped when a white-coated doctor poked his head around the curtain that gave me a semblance of privacy. "It appears you're feeling much better," he commented. "I could hear you in the hall."

"We'll wait outside," Charlotte said, tugging Ben away from the bed. "We just wanted to come by and see if you needed anything."

"She'll need a ride home in a few hours," the doctor said. "I need to run a few more tests then I think she can be released."

"You guys don't have to come back," I said. "I can take a cab home. No problem."

Ben shook his head. "Call me and I'll come get you. I feel bad I gave you the wrong impression about Fitz, Jane. I really am. Call me."

He was so contrite my anger seeped away. "I'm as much to blame as you are." I extended my hand and he gently squeezed it.

Even that was too much pressure. I quickly withdrew my hand and turned my attention to the doctor. Ben and Charlotte took the hint and left.

The doctor pulled over a computer tucked into the corner, perched on a roller cart. "Let's check your stats and make sure I'm not being overly optimistic."

****

He was optimistic, by about four hours. It took that long for test results to come back and paperwork to be processed. But by nine that night Ben was driving me back to my house. "Where's Charlotte tonight?" I asked, trying not to dirty Ben's pristine little sedan. I neglected to ask him to bring me any clean clothes, so I was dressed in my smoke-stained shorts and T-shirt and filthy garden clogs.

"She has a Tuesday and Thursday night seminar. She canceled it the other night to be home with me." Ben glanced quickly at me in the darkness, his concerned face lit by his dashboard lights. "I'm sorry about what happened, Jane. I explained it to Fitz but I'm afraid he doesn't understand."

I leaned my head cautiously against the window. "I'm afraid he does," I said softly. "I rushed to accuse him without the facts. I'm such a jerk sometimes."

"He said you had a printed copy of one of the files." Ben reached into his shirt pocket and pulled out a small memory stick. "Here's a copy of the files. Fitz thought you might want to compare the printed copy to the handwritten one. He thought there might be a discrepancy."

I took the memory stick but didn't put it into my grimy shorts pocket. Lord knows what smoke residue might do to a sensitive computer device. "I'll check it tomorrow," I said. "I think I'll take a pain pill tonight and hope the world looks like a better place in the morning."

We were silent for several miles then Ben said, "Are you going to Mr. Collins' funeral? There isn't any visitation beforehand, just a service. It's at the funeral home, not a church. You know the one, it's in that gray Victorian house on the corner near City Hall."

I thought wearily of what I would have to do to get ready for such an ordeal. "I should go," I finally said. "He cared about that fen and the wildlife refuge. It's the least I can do." I touched my head gingerly. "I need to get a haircut before then, though."

"Just wear a scarf or something. Nobody will notice."

I would have laughed if I wasn't so exhausted. Not notice someone who appeared thoroughly sunburned with singed hair to boot? I doubted I would pass unremarked. "I'll worry about it in the morning," I said around a yawn. "I'll worry about everything tomorrow."

"Fitz?" Ben asked softly.

A tear made its way down my cheek, stinging my sensitive skin. "I'm not sure there's anything to worry about there." I managed a wry smile. "Maybe if they lock me up, I'll get a chance to see him, at least."

Ben pulled into the driveway. "I'll talk to him again. Maybe I can make him understand."

"Understand what? That I thought the worst of him?"

"It's just that I'm worried about you. It seemed like he was too good to be true. I mean, well, you know what I mean."

I touched his hand. "Don't worry about it, Ben." I opened the car door and pulled my key chain from my pocket. Powdery soot came along with it. "First order of business is to get rid of these clothes," I muttered. I leaned over but couldn't bend too far without making a headache flare into life. "I'll see you at the funeral tomorrow."

"Want me to pick you up?"

"No, that's okay. I'll have to go to campus anyway. I need to cancel classes and make sure the students have their assignments for the weekend."

"Can't somebody else do that?"

"I can do it. I'll see you there tomorrow." I managed to make my way to my front door without falling and got the key into the lock. Persuasion greeted me with insistent meows. I answered his needs first then I peeled off my clothes and stood in the shower, rinsing off the smell of smoke mingled with hospital. I carried my dirty clothes to the garbage and dropped them in, then ate a cracker, took a pill, and fell into bed.

Chapter 11

I didn't sleep well despite the drugs. I tossed and turned and every time I did, something hurt. Either my hand, or my arm, or my face, or my back, or my legs. I couldn't get comfortable and after dozing for a few hours, I finally got up.

I wandered into the kitchen and made myself a cup of coffee. Persuasion and I went to the porch and curled up on the chaise lounge, covered by an old afghan. I watched the sun rise while my brain dredged up every nuance of every conversation I had with Fitz.

It didn't help. Nothing made sense anymore. I had no idea who killed Mrs. Burge. I didn't know if the missing will was really missing, I wasn't sure if those files that Mr. Collins gave me had any value. All I knew was I hurt, body and soul, and I had to get off my butt and face the day.

I went in to the bathroom to take stock of what I had to work with. I tried a few scarves, but nothing seemed right. Finally I took my scissors and cut the worst of the burnt spots on my head. That left me with a raggedy sort of boy-cut. It would have to do. I gave up and took another shower, this time luxuriating in the massaging warmth.

When I emerged I felt as though I'd shed a layer of skin and some of my burdens. Whatever would happen with Fitz, it would happen, no matter how I worried about it. I couldn't control anything whatsoever about the police investigation, so I would have to let that play out as it would. And I had no clue about the missing will or why Mrs. Burge told me she had changed hers.

I fixed a bowl of cereal and went into my study. I spied the memory stick on the desk and brought up the list of files. I munched my corn flakes and skimmed through the list, pausing occasionally to peer at one of the scanned images. About halfway through the list I found two files in a sub-directory named JANE_VIEW.

"Well, that's plain enough, I guess," I muttered. I opened the sub-directory and clicked open the two images in it.

One was a copy of Samuel Collins' will. It was dated five years earlier and in it he designated Luke Collins as his beneficiary with a few other bequests to other people, one of whom was George Wick, who stood to inherit the house and the land where it sat. I printed the four-page document.

Odd. A person couldn't make a bequest to his attorney, could he? Wouldn't that be a conflict of interest or something? Detective Forster said a will was dated ten years earlier. This one would override that one, surely. Wouldn't it? And according to Mrs. Burge, she made an even more recent one, too.

I jotted a note on my desktop To Do list to check my will and make sure it was current. I hadn't revised mine as often as Mr. Collins did, apparently. I wondered if Fitz had seen that document, then I remembered that of course he did. He put it into a folder for me to see, so surely he had already reviewed it.

But that made no sense, either. Ann said that Fitz

had reviewed the documents and didn't find a will. She also said he found nothing of any value. Did Fitz just not tell her about it? Or was she lying?

The other file was the handwritten version of the chronological list I used at the SOFT meeting, a week earlier. I dug out the typed version and printed the handwritten one and spent a laborious fifteen minutes comparing the two.

Fitz was right. There were discrepancies between them. The handwritten list had several extra notations around those missing deed dates. The writing was small and cramped and even after magnifying the image several times, I couldn't decipher what was written. It appeared to be notes with initials and a word that might be 'check' or something like it. The initials were either LAC or EAC. It was hard to tell which. Some initials seemed like AAB or maybe WB, and in a couple of spots it appeared that yet a third set of initials was used, either GU or AU.

I printed the handwritten version and when I got up to retrieve it from my printer, I saw it was almost seven-thirty. I had a lot to accomplish before a ten o'clock funeral. I shut down my computer and hurriedly got dressed for the day, choosing dark slacks and a white on navy starred shirt, which I decided was somber enough for a summer funeral.

I dabbed on some powder but I didn't dare try liquid makeup. My skin was still too sensitive. The bruise on my face couldn't be hid no matter what, but the powder did help tone down the livid purple color. I considered some eye shadow but decided it might clash with the garish bruise, so I settled on mascara and lipstick and called it done.

I made another stab at working on my hair, but other than slicking it down with water, I couldn't do much with it. I managed to get it to mostly lie down, but it was so thick it still felt like it was ready to spring up into clumps at any moment. I would need a real hairstyle in a week or two, once enough had grown back to be styled.

I swept up the memory stick, my SOFT notebook, and the printed pages. I jammed everything into my book bag and I was gone by eight-thirty. I felt surprisingly refreshed and energized although I still felt like I had a sunburn, and it was odd not to have hair swinging around my face when I moved.

I drove past the remains of the Burge home, driving at a crawl while I gawked at the shocking relic of the once gorgeous showplace. The roof and walls were still intact, but the interior of the house appeared to be a shell with dark streaks of dirt and soot around the windows and doors. The pristine green lawn was a mess, too, with deep tire tracks gouged into it and the ruts full of muddy water. The smell of wet smoke hung around the place, and I thought I saw a tendril of smoke in the back where something might still be smoldering.

I drove to campus and worked with the secretary to prepare assignments for my students which would keep them busy over the weekend. She promised to deliver them to my three Friday classes, and by nine thirty I was done there and heading to the funeral home near City Hall.

I parked in the lot next to the gray Victorian mansion with blue shutters and went inside the cool, dark interior. A woman greeted me in the foyer and handed me a small program before ushering me toward a room on the right. A small table at the front held several pictures arrayed on a bulletin board, and I paused to examine them.

I barely recognized Mr. Collins in most of them. I had only known him as elderly and somewhat infirm, but in the pictures he was a strapping young man, his arm around a slender woman. He and the woman were both young with the smiling, carefree optimism of youth, a couple just starting their lives together. In one picture he had an axe in his hand and a pile of firewood at his feet. It reminded me of Fitz, which reminded me of how badly I had hurt him, which made me wipe away a tear. Another photo, badly wrinkled, showed Collins and several other men in military uniforms standing before what were the ruins of a bomb site, rubble behind them.

In two pictures he stood with a small child, probably his son, Luke. Neither of them appeared happy to be there, but the little boy mustered a smile, at least. In one of them a little girl was in the background, watching them. The picture was faded and the color was bad, but I think it was Ann Burge, her hair bright red and long.

The pictures made me realize how little I knew about Mr. Collins and his life. I always thought of him as the grumpy old man who lived down the street, but here was another story that I think would have been interesting to know. How true of so many people. Stories and histories abounded that no one else knew about. Look at Mrs. Burge and the story she told about the young couple, possibly killed by their own families. Who knew such tragedy existed in the lives of people I knew?

I turned away from the picture display and saw Ann Burge, stopped in the doorway and staring at me. She wore a dark green dress and carried a matching handbag. For an instant I was reminded of her mother and the purse Mrs. Burge carried the day she died.

We locked eyes but she didn't reveal anything about how she felt. What was she doing there? Her mother had just died. Shouldn't she be home, in mourning? Did Ann know that it was my garden tool that killed her mother? Ann came into the room and went to speak to the minister who sat at the front near a small podium, smiling benignly at those who had assembled.

Chairs were set up for fifty or so visitors and a handful of people were already seated. I spied some of the SOFT committee members as well as neighbors from our subdivision and I joined them on the far side of the room, near the front. I hurriedly explained my appearance to the others, mentioning that Mrs. Burge had died in the fire but not how she died. That created a buzz of conversation that almost drowned out the recorded music droning in the background.

George Wick entered the room and started toward me, but I shot him a *back off* glare and he took the hint, detouring to a seat at the back. His black eye had apparently healed because he didn't seem any different to me. He was still rumpled and disheveled. As though offsetting George's appearance, Fitz came into the room. His pressed dark pants, crisp blue shirt, and striped tie appeared expensive, and his dark shoes seemed to glow with color. He took a seat on the opposite side of the room and behind me, just out of my peripheral vision. Before he sat, he and George exchanged frosty nods.

A few minutes later Ben and Charlotte arrived. Charlotte sat behind me, and Ben went to the front to talk to the minister, who was escorting Ann to a spot in the front row with the *Reserved for Family* sign. "How do you feel?" Charlotte whispered. "I'm surprised to see you up and moving."

I twisted left in my chair to talk to her, intercepting a stare from Fitz as I did so. I smiled and he nodded once then examined the program in his hands. "I feel better," I told Charlotte. "I think I look worse than I feel."

"You seem better today, but that bruise is really bad. Don't overdo it."

"Not to worry. I canceled classes for the day and once this service is over, I'll go home and sit back and relax. I have no plans for anything strenuous for the next few days."

"Good." Charlotte leaned closer. "I talked to Fitz. I don't think he's angry, but you did hurt his feelings, I think. But—" She leaned closer still. "I'll be honest. I think it's done him some good to discover that not everyone automatically believes he's a saint. Everything has always come easy for him. It's not a terrible thing for him to have to prove himself."

Ben joined Charlotte. "I like your hair that way."

"Anything is an improvement, right?" I turned back to face the front, once again trading glances with Fitz. This time he smiled faintly, one corner of his mouth quirking up. I took that as a good sign. Or at least a sign. I wasn't sure what kind.

A dozen or so other people straggled in, and at ten o'clock the minister stood and addressed the small assembly. "Thank you for attending this celebration of remembrance for Samuel Collins, who died unexpectedly on June 11 of this year. His son, Luke, cannot be with us today because he was injured in a tragic fire as he tried to rescue a woman trapped inside the burning house. Luke requested that the service go on without him." The minister sounded like he disapproved of this, but he was soldiering on at the insistence of a son who was making poor decisions in the throes of grief.

The minister launched into a summary of Mr. Collins' life, the typical sort of biography always given at funerals, with dates for marriage, children, jobs, and so on. My mind wandered, bouncing from thought to thought. Mrs. Burge stated that she would testify in court that Mr. Collins wanted the land to be donated. Mr. Collins' death was an accident. Mrs. Burge was murdered, or so it appeared. Fitz thought George was defrauding his clients.

Mr. Collins created a new will. Did George know that? I couldn't steal a peek at George since he sat directly behind me. George might have killed Mr. Collins in order to inherit the house. But that didn't make sense. Mr. Collins died in the fen, near the wildlife refuge. No one else was there. The police didn't suspect murder. But maybe now that Mrs. Burge was dead, they might reopen their investigation into Mr. Collins' death. I gave up speculating on that avenue of thought and switched gears.

The initials I saw on that document. Maybe it wasn't AU, but GW. The way Mr. Collins formed his letters, his elaborate penmanship might make a W like a U. What about the other initials? Did they have any

When the minister asked us to pray, I dipped my head and used that action to peek over my left shoulder. Fitz was only a dozen or so seats away, and he appeared to be devoutly praying. But just as the minister intoned an *Amen,* Fitz glanced at me. The light reflected off his glasses so I couldn't see his expression, but I thought he seemed sad. Of course, it was appropriate for a funeral, but maybe it had to do with me. Or maybe not. Who knew?

I pretended to be fiddling with my raggedy hair, hiding my face from his gaze. I swore I could feel his eyes on me while the minister recited a few Bible verses, which I suppose made some kind of sense, at least according to the minister. I have always had a hard time with the Bible since the meaning often seemed convoluted. Of course, many people feel that way about Shakespeare, whom I found perfectly understandable. To each his own, I suppose.

The minister looked at Ann when he wrapped up his sermonizing. She walked to the podium appearing perfectly composed in her fitted dress and matching high-heeled pumps. A slight buzz broke out as people whispered to each other while she faced the crowd, hands clasped in front of her.

Ann closed her eyes briefly, as though gathering strength. "Thank you for coming today. Luke asked me to speak because he was injured in the fire that killed my mother." She wiped at her eyes and took a deep, shuddering sigh.

The crowd went perfectly still, many of them anxiously waiting for her to break down and cry. Maybe I was a cynic, but I didn't think that would happen. When I witnessed Ann and her mother arguing, I saw a depth of dislike between the two of them that stretched back for years. If anything, Ann was probably feeling relief.

A small thought niggled at the back of my brain. Ann feeling relief. Ann getting revenge on her mother. Ann getting revenge...

"I knew the family well," Ann continued. "We grew up together, I suppose you could say." She told a few anecdotes, stories of Mr. Collins and Luke. From the way she talked you wouldn't have known her family was embroiled in a bitter lawsuit that stretched on for decades. According to her, they lived a bucolic and happy life gathering wildflowers and playing hide and seek among the trees in the fen. I suppose it was crass of me to be critical since the woman had just lost her mother in a rather brutal fashion. But I think that was why I was so critical. Shouldn't she be home mourning? Shouldn't she be crying instead of standing there like a model getting ready to strut the catwalk?

Ann returned to her seat after a mercifully short speech, then Ben stood, edging past Charlotte to go to the front of the gathering. He talked about SOFT and how Mr. Collins was so involved in the organization, and about Mr. Collins' love for the fen and his concerns for the environment. Ann seemed peeved at that, but all she could do was listen to him and fidget.

"He cared so much for the neighborhood and the wildlife refuge that he donated his papers to the organization. We hope to learn much from the historical record of the area and we hope to be able to carry on his work and see that the land he cared about so dearly is preserved for future generations."

I caught sight of Ann when Ben said that. I thought she might get sick. Her face paled and she leaned forward, like someone in pain or distress. She was seated ahead of me and on my left, and she turned to regard me. When she saw me watching her, she frowned as though puzzled and turned back to the minister, who took Ben's place at the front of the gathering.

The minister closed the service with another prayer, then people started to leave, heading for the next room where coffee and cookies were being served. I stood to leave but the people around me were slow movers. Consequently I was easy prey for George, who hurried forward to stand in front of me, preventing me from leaving the row of chairs.

"I'm surprised to see you here today," he said, not bothering to lower his voice. "I heard you had a bit of a disagreement with the police."

A few of the exiting people paused. Ben and Charlotte hesitated near the door, and Ann Burge, standing just a few feet away, didn't bother to pretend disinterest. I felt like I was in a spotlight, and my skin, already painfully burned, got hotter with embarrassment. Pain usually makes me angry, and the futility and injustice I'd been experiencing boiled up in me and threatened to spill over.

"What you know can be put on the head of a pin, George," I snapped. "In fact, if snot were brains, you couldn't blow your nose."

"Very aptly said." Fitz's amused voice came from my left. He had approached us via the row ahead of me and he now stood close by, watching. "I'm Miss Austin's attorney, so if you care to make any other disparaging remarks, feel free to do so. We welcome any witnesses to any slander you might try to perpetrate." He emphasized the word *attorney* and George glared at him.

"That's right," I said with a sweet smile. "I forgot. You're a lawyer, aren't you, George? Fitz is an attorney. Did you draw up Mr. Collins' will, George?"

"It is perfectly legal in the state of Iowa for a lawyer to assist clients with legal matters." George tried hard to sound distinguished and pompous, but it ended up sounding whiny. He just didn't have the mien to pull off distinguished.

Fitz did, though. "Assist, yes," he said. "File the official papers? No." Fitz put his hand over mine where it rested on the back of the chair in the row where he stood. "That's what was wrong with that list you showed me. The dates for deeds and filings and why some of the entries were blank."

I peered up at him, not understanding. He stared at me, and I knew he was willing me to trust him, willing me to follow along with his lead. "Of course," I lied. "Now it makes sense."

George's bloodshot eyes widened. "What are you talking about? What list are you talking about? I heard that Mr. Collins' legal papers were stolen." He glanced past me. I turned and saw Ann, who stood just a few feet away, listening.

"They were," she said, stepping forward. "That's what I was told, at least. Luke mentioned it."

Fitz's hand tightened over mine. I bit back an *ouch* at the pressure. "Mr. Collins gave Jane some documents and she retained one of them, which she needed for her talk to the town council last week. We never had a chance to compare them to the documents that were stolen. Ben and I were going to review the legal files, but they were taken before we could."

George visibly relaxed. "Oh, I see. I suppose it's a good thing, then, that I have his will on file and a few of the other more important land documents."

I struggled to keep my jaw from dropping. "You do?" I managed to croak.

Fitz's hand lightened on mine. "Would you mind if we glance through them?" He smiled at me then at George, seemingly casual. "Is there a chronological record of land sales included in what you have? The police asked Jane about it yesterday, when we talked."

"You spoke with the police?" Ann asked, moving around the chairs to stand next to George in the now empty room. "About what?"

I eyed her suspiciously. "Didn't the police tell you how your mother died?"

She drew back in surprise. "She died in the fire."

George grinned. "There's more to it than that." He smirked at Fitz. "Do you want to tell her or should I?"

Fitz shrugged. "I don't care. Before you do, though, would you let Jane sit down? She's been injured and she needs to rest."

I started to protest but Fitz shook his head. I sank back into my chair, playing the part of the wounded heroine. Fitz pushed past George and sat down next to me on my right, taking my hand and holding it like I was some invalid aunt. "Go ahead, George," Fitz said. "Tell Ann what you think is going on."

George hesitated, his red-rimmed eyes studying Fitz. "From what I was told, the police suspect that Jane had a hand in your mother's death, Ann."

I drew breath to protest, but Fitz did it for me. "That's incorrect." He regarded Ann, who had moved to stand in front of us, in the row of chairs ahead of me. "The police did indeed find a garden tool of Jane's at the scene."

"At the scene?" George gave a disbelieving snort. "Buried in Mrs. Burge's body, you mean."

I winced, expecting a similar reaction from Ann. Instead she just seemed puzzled. "I thought she died in the fire," she murmured. "Are you saying someone killed her?" Ann's attention riveted on me. "You did it? Why? Do you really want the land that much? You heard what my mother said about her will. Did you think you could kill her and that would stop the construction project?" Her voice started to rise.

I started to rise, too, but Fitz put his arm around me and held me in place. Ann's glare switched to him. He returned her furious glare with one of calm impassivity. "Jane had nothing to do with your mother's death and the police know that. They're investigating arson and also a possible connection to your mother's murder."

Ann stepped back, bumping into one of the folding chairs. "What?"

Fitz nodded. "They're executing a search warrant right now, I believe. They're checking for fire accelerants at your house and the Collins home." He glanced at me. "They'll want to go through your house for propane."

"I don't have any," I said. "I use a charcoal grill. I'm old-fashioned."

He smiled. "So am I."

"I have a gas grill." Ann's voice was shrill, panicked. "That doesn't mean anything."

"Of course it does," Fitz said confidently. "The police can match the type of propane used at the fire with the propane remaining in any tank. It's one of those forensic tests they can do."

Ann backed away. "I don't believe you."

Fitz shrugged. "I don't know the details. I'm not a criminal attorney. But I have friends who are, and that's what I was told." He turned his attention to George. "Would you mind if we dropped by your office to examine the legal documents Mr. Collins left with you? The police might be interested in them, too."

Now it was George's turn to appear panicked. "No, that's fine. I'll just, I'll—I have to get back right now, but perhaps later they can stop."

"In an hour?" Fitz asked. "That should work for us, right, Jane?" He looked down at me, his dark brown eyes insistent.

I nodded. "Sure," I mumbled, not sure what I was agreeing to. "Whatever Fitz says."

"Perfect. We'll convene at your office in an hour then." Fitz consulted his shiny wrist watch. "Noon?"

"Sure. Good." George almost ran Ann down in his haste to leave the room. She stared at us, her blue eyes narrowed with suspicion.

"I don't believe you, Fitz," she said slowly.

Fitz regarded her with a steady gaze. "If you have nothing to hide, then there's nothing to worry about, is there?"

She nodded slowly then left the room, less quickly than George but moving with purpose.

I turned to Fitz. "What the hell just happened?"

He pulled a cell phone from his pants pocket and dialed a number. "Hold the questions for a second, okay?" He focused on the phone. "Detective Forster, please." Pause. "This is Fitzgerald Williams. Yes, I talked to him. He should be arriving any moment." Pause, listen. "Excellent. Thank you. Oh, and by the way—Ann Burge may ask you about forensic testing for propane." Pause. Fitz started to grin. "That's what I thought. You may want to verify her movements." Pause. "Thank *you,* Detective." He tucked the phone back into his pocket and turned to me. "Mission accomplished."

I stared at him. "You devious scoundrel, you," I said in admiration. "You set George up. Are the police waiting for him?"

Fitz nodded. "I suspected he stole the papers to cover up his illegal doings. George had acted as an attorney for quite a while. Any papers he supposedly filed would be null and void. He couldn't let that be exposed, so when Ann mentioned to him that you had handed the documents over to Ben, George knew what he had to do."

I sorted through the speculations bouncing in my brain. "The propane?"

"Totally bogus. I have no idea how the fire was set, but the police are sure Mrs. Burge died from something other than the wound to her chest. I think they'll find she died, your tool was used to divert suspicion, and the fire was set to attempt to cover up everything."

"And to destroy any papers she had," I said, remembering the argument between the woman and Ann. "Mrs. Burge said she had copies of important papers, too."

"I couldn't figure out why she was killed. But that makes sense."

"And to get back at me. Revenge. Ann wants revenge. Ann has always disliked me, and I have no idea why." I sat back. "You're one hell of a lawyer."

"Attorney," he corrected. "And don't you forget it." He gently touched my bruised face. "All I did was to help you."

I was once again struck by how good he looked in dress clothes. I had never known a man who dressed so well or who wore his clothes so well. It was a bit intimidating. Well, the hell with that. I wouldn't worry about a stupid thing like how rich he was or how he dressed. I took the plunge. "I screwed up. I know I did. I misunderstood Ben."

He took my hand and touched the burns on my palms very gently. His eyelashes were dark on his cheeks and he seemed hesitant or unsure. "For some reason I feel that you are predisposed to believe the worst of me." He stared into my eyes and I saw puzzled hurt in his. "Why?" I started to speak but he shook his head. "Why?" he repeated.

I forced myself to face what I'd been running from since he first asked me out on that ill-fated date where we had the run-in with George Wick. "I think you must be slumming. You're rich, you're upper-class, you're East Coast. I'm not rich, I'm middle-class, and I'm Midwest. I'm not stylish, I don't have a degree from Bryn Mawr or Sarah Lawrence and I don't know a Riesling from a Chardonney except I know I like Riesling better." I pulled my hand away from his. "I'm not the right person for you."

He nodded as though completely unsurprised by what I said. "That's what I thought. You're prejudiced. You're a snob."

My jaw dropped. "I am not."

"You are. You're assuming that because I come from a different background than you that I'm snobbish and I look down on you." Fitz held up a hand when I tried to speak. "I admit, my book review was unbearably condescending and if I could do it over, I would. I would still be honest, but I'd reconsider how I phrased it. But think of your interactions with me. Have I ever indicated in any way that I think you're lesser than me?"

"You—I—" I couldn't remember an example. His brown eyes were so hypnotic I was paralyzed.

"It's true my family is wealthy and has a great deal of influence in certain circles. That's irrelevant. It's true I am relatively well-off but I believe the only indication of that I have shown is my choice of a car which is somewhat expensive for a college professor. I confess I have a love of fine dining and fine wine and I offer no apology for that. I can afford to buy what I want and I do, but I don't flaunt it in any way."

"But you're—" I stopped, not sure what I wanted to say. He waited patiently, watching me as I sought words. "It does not make any sense that you would care about me. I just don't understand it."

"You're inventing reasons to not trust me. You're inventing reasons to not love me." Fitz kept his eyes on my face, pinning me to my chair.

"Now that's arrogant. I'm just trying to be practical. We have nothing in common."

"We have more in common than you will acknowledge. I don't care about your background and I don't care about your supposed lack of style. You are smart, witty, loving, and loyal. I believe those are qualities I possess as well. You're well-read, you love to garden, and you don't mind getting dirty."

"Are you serious?" I stared into his eyes and saw only sincerity there. "I may be a romance author, but I'm not real good at the romance stuff myself." I made a leap of faith. "I'm willing to try, though, if you are."

Fitz stood and pulled me up off my feet and to him in a breath-stopping hug. "Dear God, when I saw you in that hospital bed—" His chest heaved under my cheek. "You were so small, so bruised and hurt. I wanted to kill whoever set that fire and put you in danger."

"Are you sure?" I asked, slipping my arms around him. "I might embarrass you when you introduce me to your family."

"I am not worried about my family or any antiquated idea about what is socially correct. You are more than my equal, Jane. Believe me."

I pulled slowly away from him. "That's it. The family. Socially correct. That's it."

"That's what?" He touched my hair tentatively. "I think you'll have to cut it shorter, but I think it would look fine on you."

"The wills. I know where they are." I moved away from him, thinking furiously, little facts and words falling into place.

Chapter 12

"What wills?" Fitz started walking toward the doorway, keeping his arm firmly around my shoulders.

I slipped an arm around his waist, happy to keep close to him. "Mrs. Burge told me that she and Mr. Collins revised their wills recently. She also said that they kept a copy of them in a safe place."

Fitz nodded. "I advised them both to have new wills made."

"When did you do that?"

"Months ago. When I first came to town. I was talking to Mrs. Burge at an event that Ann and I were attending. When she discovered I was an attorney, she asked for my help." He frowned thoughtfully. "She specifically asked that I not tell Ann about it."

I nodded excitedly. "That's it. That has to be the newest will. I wonder what attorney they used. Wait a minute. She said something about ceding the land now with a provision that it be made permanent. Did you tell her about that?"

Fitz nodded. "Mrs. Burge was certain her will might be contested. She wanted to do something now, rather than wait."

"But Mr. Collins didn't do that. I wonder why he didn't."

Fitz stilled. "Perhaps he did," he said.

"What?"

"Those documents. Maybe there's something in there. Maybe it's one of the handwritten items that Ben didn't scan. We can only hope that George didn't destroy everything he didn't think was valuable. There might be useful information there."

"None of that may matter. I'm sure I know where the wills are kept." I thought of the flash of red I saw in the woods that day, the glimpse of a ribbon on a tree. "I'm sure of it. Mrs. Burge told me about it before she died. She didn't say anything until after Ann left, so I'm betting Ann doesn't know about it." I hurried ahead, slipping away from him.

"Where are you going?"

"I just need to check something real quick."

"Where?"

"At the fen. There's a tree there and I think—" I laughed shakily. "Talk about a romance plot. It's a long story."

"I'll go with you." I started to protest but he just shook his head. "There is no way I am letting you go into danger without me. It's bad enough you ran into a burning building yesterday. What were you thinking of?" He held open the door for me and we emerged into the brilliant June sunshine.

"It seemed like a good idea at the time," I admitted, heading for my car. Ann's red sports car was near it, like a starlet next to my stodgy little sedan.

He took my arm and steered me in the opposite direction. "We'll come back for your car. Let's leave it here in case George or anyone else is keeping tabs on you."

"Good idea," I said admiringly. "Are you sure you weren't a criminal lawyer?"

Pried

"I didn't say I was never a criminal attorney. I just said I wasn't one at present. I was a public defender for three years before I switched to contract law." Fitz smiled at me, deep dimples echoing his mischievous eyes. "You have to remember, Jane, I'm accustomed to legal tactics. There are varieties of truth. It just depends on the circumstance." I stopped, and he walked a step further before realizing I wasn't keeping pace. "What is it? What's wrong?"

"I don't know if I agree with that statement."

He rejoined me, staring into my eyes. "I will always be totally honest with you, Jane. Is that what concerns you?"

I tried to find a tactful way to express my doubts, but finally just settled on the blatant truth. "I don't know if I like the idea of being with a man who might be cleverer than me."

Fitz cradled my face in his hands. "Jane, there are different sorts of clever just as there are shades of truth. Trust me when I say I believe you are far cleverer than me in the ways that matter." He lowered his face and our lips met in a kiss.

My arms went around him and I fell into the moment, abandoning any pretense of detachment or hesitation. This man had me heart and soul with his honesty, his humor, and his damn sense of fair play. For the first time in my life, I felt like I had finally met my equal.

When we separated, I clung to him for one more long moment. He didn't speak but just held me, my burned face pressed to his chest. I finally looked up at him. "This is scary," I whispered. "When did you become so important to me?"

He laughed shakily. "About the same time the same thing happened to me, I guess."

I moved away from him but kept my arm hooked through his. "Let's make sure nothing goes wrong," I said. "I want a chance to enjoy this."

"Agreed."

We went to the back of the funeral home parking lot where Fitz's pearl gray sedan sat. "This is a gorgeous car," I said, settling into the soft leather seats. Everything around me that wasn't trimmed in walnut was either pale gray or black.

"I like it better than the Jaguar," he said, easing the car into gear and backing up. "The Jag doesn't handle as well."

"You owned a Jaguar?" That entire class of car was so far out of my price range it may as well have been a space shuttle.

"My father did." He focused on the road, shifting gears effortlessly. "Where's the best place to find this hiding spot? Should I go to your house?"

I considered it. If I was right, the wills were hidden in the tree used as a lover's mailbox. The simplest way to get there was through the fen, on the walkway behind the Collins house. But I wasn't sure if it was the safest route to take. "Is Luke Collins still in the hospital?"

"I'm not sure. Why?"

"Go to my house and you can park in my garage," I said. "If Ann is home then she won't see your car. If Luke is home, we'll need to find a different way to the spot."

"If my ruse worked, she's busily getting rid of any propane she owns." Fitz smiled. "I enjoyed that little misdirection, I must admit."

"You sounded totally honest, too. You're good at lying." I felt a faint qualm when I said it, but it was the truth.

"I didn't lie. A colleague of mine did tell me something like that once. Of course, we were both drunk at the time and I didn't believe him, but if Ann believed me…" He shrugged. "So be it."

I barely heard him. I was trying to remember the area around the big oak tree. I hadn't walked through the fen that often and wasn't as familiar with it as Mr. Collins was. But if I recalled correctly, the wooden walkway did go near that tree, which stood on the outskirts of the fen. Or we could go through the pasture and presumably approach the tree from the hillside. I hadn't ever gone into the pasture, just drove by it or walked past it. We'd have to decide when we got there.

A few minutes later Fitz drove into my driveway and I hopped out and opened the garage door for him. He parked inside then joined me. "This way," I said, going into the house.

"I thought we were going to the marsh." Fitz followed me through the garage access door, through the living room, and to the porch at the back. Persuasion bounded from the study to greet me, saw Fitz, and bounded back again.

"He doesn't like strangers," I explained, unlocking the porch door. "We don't need to follow the road. We can walk through the woods down to the marsh."

"Through the woods?"

I gestured to the trees that formed a border for my yard. "Those trees go all the way to the pasture and the marsh. There are two ways to get to the spot I'm thinking of. We can go through the fen, starting at the

Collinses' back yard, or we can go through the pasture. But the only access to the pasture is from the Collins house. There's a barbed-wire fence along the road and I don't think we can easily get through there. And I know we can't get through without being seen."

"But there's no fence by the woods?" Fitz asked. "A natural barrier?"

I nodded. "We can go downhill from here, through the woods, and we'll be in the pasture. Maybe I'm being paranoid, but I don't like the idea of marching through the Collinses' back yard."

"I think it pays to be careful. Someone killed Mrs. Burge."

Holy buckets. He was right. I had completely forgotten that in my quest to find the wills. "Okay then. The woods it is. Oh. Wait." I kicked off my sandals and went into my bedroom via the French doors on the porch.

Fitz followed me, stopping when he saw where we were. "What are you doing?"

I rummaged in the closet and emerged with a pair of sneakers. "I think I need sturdier shoes." I slipped my Keds on then eyed his shiny footwear. "Your shoes will get dirty."

"Not a problem. I have other shoes." He followed me back to the porch. "You have a lovely home, by the way. I like the floor plan."

I went out the porch door, closing it carefully behind Fitz lest Persuasion decide to embark on an adventure. "I love it, too. It's small, but it suits me. Come on." I skirted my small pond and went to the woods lining the edge of my property. "These trees extend down the hill to the Collins' house," I explained, heading for the narrow deer trail, barely visible. "In theory it's an empty lot, but it's so steep no one will build on it." I ducked into the trees.

"Lead on," Fitz said behind me. "Unless you want me to break a path."

I didn't reply but moved into the small forest. It wasn't heavily treed so the underbrush was deep and lush. We had to move carefully because the trail wove through the trees on the hillside, with an occasional steep drop or slide where deer could run but humans had to grope their way. Once I nearly pitched forward when I caught my foot on a fallen limb, and Fitz grabbed me, keeping me upright. I hung onto him for a minute to get my nerves back.

"Want me to go first?" he asked.

I shook my head. "I know the way better, I think. Just be careful in here. There's a drop-off coming up. A small stream runs through here, just run-off from the road, but it's cut a deep embankment. We'll have to jump it then it's downhill from there to the edge of the fen. That's where the stream feeds the marsh."

"Go slow," he said, releasing me. "We have plenty of time."

I nodded, reluctant to leave the safety of his arms. I moved forward, keeping my eyes focused on the ground in front of me. This was typical Iowa woodland with a mixture of oak, basswood, hickory, and maples interspersed with low-growing shrubs like gooseberry and choke cherry. My main concerns were the footing and any thorny protuberances on errant branches and scouting for poison ivy, which I was certain was there somewhere.

The ground underfoot began to slant crazily

downward. "Be careful here," I said. "The stream is right ahead." I pushed forward cautiously, using a fallen branch to part the shrubs in front of me. Sure enough the ground dropped off a dozen feet or more to the winding trickle below us. "We can follow this down to the fen from here," I said.

"They weren't kidding when they called you Nature Girl," Fitz said.

I glanced back at him. He had rolled up his shirt sleeves, and his necktie stuck out of his back pocket. Burrs stuck to his dress pants, and sweat stains showed under his arms. "I'm sorry. I suppose we could have used the road, but I wasn't sure how to get there without going through the Collinses' yard."

He came alongside me to peer down at the stream. "I don't mind a little tramp in the woods. How do we get across?"

I pointed to the left. "There's a tree. Six steps and you're across." I led the way to the upturned hickory tree which had fallen over to the other bank. A large part of the trunk spanned the stream, but it took a lot of scrambling over branches to get to a place where we could climb up on the trunk.

"Ready?" I asked Fitz.

He looked doubtfully at the broad tree then at the stream below. "Seriously?"

I nodded. "It's okay. Just keep your eyes straight ahead and walk slowly. The trunk is pretty stable."

"Pretty stable?"

"Watch." I climbed up on the trunk and took two steps forward. "It only bounces a little bit. Just wait until I'm over, then come on." I continued forward, arms outstretched to keep my balance. It was only a ten-foot walk, and the trunk was relatively broad and easy to balance on. I got to the other side and carefully turned. "Come on."

Fitz got onto the trunk, staring down at the stream. "I should perhaps tell you that I don't like heights."

I didn't either, but I didn't mention that. "Just a few steps," I encouraged.

He nodded and took a tentative step forward then stopped.

"Look at me." I snapped my fingers. "Eyes on me, Fitz."

His head jerked up and he stared intently at me. "Okay," he said. "I can do this."

"I know you can. One more step. Come on." He slid his left foot forward. "Okay, one more. You can do it." Slowly, inch by inch, he made his way over the trunk until he was finally just a foot away. "Okay, just one more step, you can do it." I held out my hand and he took it, hurrying ahead so quickly his momentum sent us crashing into the underbrush.

I kept my feet but scraped my already burnt arm on a tree that sent waves of pain crashing into me. I would have dropped to my knees, but Fitz kept his arms around me, holding me upright. "I'm sorry," he murmured. "I'm so sorry. I hurt you."

I held on tight, willing the pain to subside. "It's okay. We're almost there. We can walk back by the road, okay? No more climbing around in the woods."

"Deal." He stared down into my face. "You know, if you're having plot problems in your book, just have your heroine take the hero for a walk in the woods. I think she'll manage to assume a leadership role."

"Good idea."

We stood for a moment then I broke away. "Okay, I think the pasture shouldn't be too far now. These woods border it on the north. From there we'll have to walk through the field, but if we stay to the left, I think we'll be below the hill line and no one would see us from the road."

"What about the Collins house?"

"I'm not so sure about that," I admitted. "It's up on a small hill. We'll just have to take our chances, I think."

"Okay. We've come this far." He touched my fire-ravaged head. "Lead on, scout."

I paused to get my bearings, then I moved to my right, heading back to the path we'd been following, which continued on this side of the stream. It took another five minutes of scrambling, but soon we saw the cleared field ahead.

"Where are we going?" Fitz asked while we stood in the shadows of the trees, the horse and donkey grazing in the distance.

I pointed to the tall oak, the red ribbon fluttering from its branches. "That tree. Mrs. Burge said that it used to be used like a post office when she was a child. Both she and Mr. Collins knew about it. I'm betting they hid their documents there."

"That makes as much sense as anything. Let's go."

It felt dreadfully exposed to emerge from the woods. The distance was only a football field length, maybe slightly more, but it was hilly and uneven going so it seemed to take forever. Finally we approached the tree which towered over the other trees that bordered the marshy ground which marked the start of the wetlands.

"Where do you think it is?" Fitz asked, walking around the tree and peering up at it.

"It has to be someplace where a person can easily reach it," I said. "Mrs. Burge said that when they were children, they used to hide notes here." I didn't mention the story of the tragic lovers. Ann was right about one thing. That was in the past and best left there.

Fitz walked around the tree, keeping one hand on the trunk when the ground sloped away, leading to the marshlands. "I don't see anything."

I leaned back, looking up for any nook or notch where things could be stored. I tried to imagine myself as a child, tucking a note into a spot where it could be seen to those who knew where to find it. I reached up, touching the bark of the old trunk while I walked slowly around the tree, using the visible roots to give me a boost.

That's when I felt it. The nook wasn't immediately visible unless you were tall, but I felt it when I ran my hand over the bark. I guess there were benefits to being short. "Here."

Fitz came to my side and watched as I strained upward, my right arm extended as far as I could. I saw a crack in the trunk, hardly visible and more easily felt. I reached inside then Fitz reached over me, his taller height allowing him to quickly extract the plastic wrapped manila file folder.

"That's it," I said, reaching for the bundle.

Fitz held it out of my reach. "No matter what happens, Jane, trust me."

"What?"

"You weren't supposed to get caught up in this. Trust me, Jane. Please." He held the plastic-wrapped folder high above me. "Promise me."

"I don't understand." I gave up straining for the folder and glared at him. "What did you do, Fitz? You're asking me to forgive you for something, aren't you?"

"Trust me." He turned away, blocking my view. "I have it!"

"You son of a bitch." I tried to pull the folder down to my level. "What did you do? What's going on?"

"Trust me."

Luke Collins came into sight from the direction of the Collins house, a gun raised level with his face and aimed at us. "Put it down," he snapped. "Now."

"I told you I'd get it," Fitz said, lowering his arm. "What's going on?"

Luke gestured with the gun and Fitz moved away from me. I was left to gape at the weapon and at Luke and Ann behind him. She still wore her funeral garb, the green dress so stylish in a cow pasture.

"What are you doing? I don't understand." I turned to Fitz, who regarded me with cool indifference.

"What does it look like? I used you to find what we needed." He stared into my eyes. "I stand to make a fortune if that road goes through. As long as we eliminate any other liens on the land, we'll make a killing."

I thought I might faint. I even swayed a bit, the world spinning around me. "You son of a bitch," I muttered. "I trusted you."

Ann moved around Luke, careful to stay away from the firing zone, or so I presumed. She took the folder from Fitz, who handed it over willingly. "You're such a fool," she said softly. "Why would you think he'd be interested in you?"

Days of accumulated anger suddenly vented. I lunged for her, my hands closing around her throat. "You damn bitch!" I shouted, pushing her to the ground. "I swear to God, I'll kill you!"

I expected Fitz or Luke to stop me, but nobody did. My hands tightened on Ann's throat then she managed to slam one hand against my face. Pain exploded in my bruised temple and I fell back. When my vision cleared, I saw her crawling toward the gun, which for some reason was on the ground. I lurched to my feet and fell on her, my knees crashing into her back. She went down like the proverbial sack of potatoes then twisted to face me, hands raised to fend me off. I raised my fist and brought it down solidly on her chin. She fell back without a sound.

I rolled off Ann, snatching up the file folder and crawling to one side to sit up. Ann lay on the ground, gasping like a beached fish, and I doubted she'd be moving anytime soon. I peered around, trying to decipher what was going on.

Fitz and Luke were locked in a struggle. The gun lay unseen on the ground, or so I assumed. Luke didn't seem injured at all. In fact, his burns were far less evident than mine. I noted that in passing when I picked up the gun from between their scuffling feet and getting tromped on in the process.

I briefly considered using it but I quickly discarded that notion. I knew nothing about firearms, and with my luck I'd shoot myself in the stomach. I tossed it as far as I could to my left, making the horse that grazed nearby glance up at the sound. It returned to perusing the grass without missing a beat.

I rolled to my right, trying to avoid the two men fighting above me. They seemed evenly matched, and Luke definitely didn't appear incapacitated by his supposed injuries. I tried to get to my feet but my head hurt so badly. Finally I gave up and lunged for Luke's legs, which weren't far from me. I missed and brought down Fitz instead, but it was okay because that allowed Fitz to toss Luke to the ground. I ended up underneath them both, struggling for air. Someone dug an elbow into my chest and I quit struggling when I passed out.

I awoke with a gasp, fighting off hands that held me down. "It's okay," someone said. "You're safe, it's okay."

I opened my eyes and found Fitz above me. His glasses were askew and it appeared that one bow had broken off. He was as disheveled as George Wick but in a handsome way, not a dissipated way. "What the hell is going on?"

"I'll explain it once you get to the hospital." He leaned over and kissed me gently.

"Hospital? Why?"

Fitz touched my face and held up his hand. I saw blood there. "You've been hurt. Let them take care of you, Jane. I'll see you there." He turned to his right and I followed his gaze.

Several men were swarming over Luke and Ann, who still lay on the ground like a lump of dead meat. "Did I kill her?" Panic made my voice louder than I meant.

One of the men looked up. It was Detective Forster. "No, you just knocked her out. Good punch."

"Oh. Good. I guess." I closed my eyes to the chaos and let darkness take me away.

****

"I used to work for the District Attorney's office in Massachusetts," Fitz said a day later. He sat in an armchair on my porch while I lounged in the chaise, Persuasion curled up near my knees. Ben and Charlotte sat on the wicker settee nearby. "When I moved here, the Derby County D.A. recruited me. They were concerned about the possibility of land fraud when it came to the construction project."

"They weren't the only ones," I grumbled. I still had not forgiven Fitz for his duplicity, but I had promised to hear him out, and I was making good on that promise. A brief hospital stay, a day's rest, and a glass of excellent wine were making it easy to do so.

"I was the perfect candidate for the job." Fitz shrugged, the picture of innocence. "I had a background in criminal investigation. I was working for Derby College, which was under scrutiny. And I had no ties to anyone in the community."

"Except Ann," I noted.

He sighed patiently. "As I explained before, she was one of the prime suspects. It was convenient when she began paying attention to me."

"Hmpf." I took a piece of bread and dipped it in the amazing artichoke dip that Fitz had brought, along with the wine. "Paying attention."

Fitz peered at me over his newly mended glasses. "Would you let me tell my story without the commentary?"

I waved a hand, but winced when my shirt sleeve interacted with my burned arm. "Go ahead," I said magnanimously. "Tell away."

"You were not supposed to get involved," he said

for maybe the dozenth time. "I tried to keep you out of it, but you insisted on playing Jessica Fletcher."

I sat up straighter on the chaise. "Jessica Fletcher? Please. Nancy Drew."

"The D.A. asked you to help," Charlotte prompted, shooting me a reproving glance. I subsided with more wine and bread smeared with artichoke dip.

"It started a few months ago. I moved to town in the fall, last year. Earlier this year Ann approached me and asked if I had plans to remain here permanently. If I did, she knew of some land that was a good price and available for purchase." Fitz leaned back in his chair and crossed his tanned legs, shown off in khaki shorts, at the ankles. "I expressed interest and she introduced me to Luke Collins."

"Did you know how much the land was worth? Did you know about the project?" I regarded my own much shorter legs, red and sunburned-looking from the fire. It would be a while before I felt comfortable in public wearing shorts. At least my hair was stylish, now in a jagged, edgy cut, easy to maintain, and which hid the worst of the burnt spots.

"I'm getting to that, Nancy Drew," Fitz said patiently. "I did some research about the project and that brought me to Mr. Collins. When it came out that I knew George, Mr. Collins asked me for legal advice. When I saw the will that George drew up, I went to the D.A. I could have gone to the police, but keep in mind that I wasn't sure who to trust. I was new to town and sometimes there can be political dealings between the police and some lawyers."

Fitz leaned over the coffee table and fixed himself a cracker and cheese before continuing. "The D.A.

explained that they had an ongoing investigation into the construction project. It's been stalled for years, but in the last year, it got new life."

"I wondered about that." I considered another dip-soaked bread piece but restrained myself. "There wasn't any funding for years, then all of a sudden it was on the list of top projects to do."

"Exactly. The D.A. is a local man and he knew the history of the project. He also knew that several people at the college were buying up land."

"So you were in the right place at the right time," Charlotte said. "At the college and now a landowner."

Fitz nodded. "Let me back up one step. No one in town questioned George's credentials. No one until I got here, that is. George knew that I would check and see if he really passed the bar exam."

"Why?" Ben asked, leaning back and putting his arm around Charlotte. They were so natural together that I had to smile.

"Because I knew George in college. He was a cheat and an asshole even then." Fitz looked at me for confirmation.

I nodded reluctantly. "I suppose everybody just assumed he was legit. He went into business with his father, and everybody trusted the old man." I turned to Ben. "You remember when he came back from college, right?"

Ben nodded. "Nobody questioned it."

"It comes down to trust," Fitz murmured, his attention on me. "George's father covered up for him for years, but after he died, it was just a matter of time until George was found out, and he knew it. That's why he pushed Mr. Collins and Mrs. Burge to include him in their wills. He didn't act as attorney of record for that filing, so it was technically legal. They were elderly, and in time, he'd inherit."

"Why didn't Ann or Luke object?" Charlotte asked.

"They might not have known. Neither child was close to the parent. They weren't even aware of the most recent wills—the ones that George engineered and the newest one, the one that I wrote."

"You wrote?" I glared at Fitz. "You didn't tell me that."

"Attorney-client confidentiality," he said. "But both are dead now, and I doubt it matters. After I spoke to Mr. Collins, he asked me to draft a new will for him. He told Mrs. Burge and she did the same. I couldn't speak about the content of the will because of the confidentiality clause. But I knew something was wrong when I saw that copy of the will in the papers stolen from Ben. Then when Mrs. Burge died, I was certain."

"I still find it hard to believe that Ann murdered her mother." Ben seemed as perplexed as me. "Is the land worth so much?"

"It wasn't just the land." I smeared more bread with dip and made a mental vow to diet tomorrow. "Ann and her mother had an ongoing feud, lasting for decades. I got a glimpse of it when they were arguing in front of me."

"I think we'll find that it was Luke who actually set the fire, but Ann who gave him the idea," Fitz said. "Ann could be very persuasive when she wanted to be."

I shot him a narrow-eyed glare. "Really?"

He smiled innocently at me. "It is more an

observation about Luke Collins than Ann. He doesn't strike me as a person with a great deal of initiative. When I purchased the land from him, I did a bit of checking on his background. His so-called ranch is just a few acres of scrubby land, a small herd of cattle, and a house. He hasn't been particularly successful."

"Was Mr. Collins murdered?" Charlotte asked. "Did Ann kill him? Jane said Mrs. Burge almost accused Ann of that."

"I don't think so," Fitz said. "I think it was truly an accident. But it was an accident that set a lot of events into motion. He died, and his son discovered that the land he was counting on selling would not be his to sell. It was either going to George Wick, according to the five-year-old will, or to the Sierra Club, if that will came to light. He contacted Ann and—"

"Ann? Why her?" I asked.

Fitz regarded me with mocking pity. "Idiot. They're lovers. I told you she would go away often on weekend jaunts. I watched how she looked at him at your house party and I knew he was the one she visited."

"How did I not know that?" I asked the world at large.

"Well, you said it yourself. You may write romance novels but you're not real good at romance." He smiled. "We'll fix that, I think."

"What's that mean?" I demanded.

"I still don't understand," Charlotte interrupted. "The D.A. was concerned about land fraud. Did you get what was needed?"

Fitz nodded. "The papers the police found at George Wick's office—the ones that were stolen from

225

Ben—have records of land purchases made over the years. Those purchases were made by people who had positions of authority at Derby College. I think you'll see a few personnel changes at the college in the coming months."

"So they bought land over the years on the expectation that the road would go through?" I sipped more wine, savoring the tart, rich flavor. Fitz really did have great taste in food and drink, I had to admit. "Isn't that a gamble?"

"Not if they're bribing elected officials to make it happen."

I stared at him, mouth agape. "Seriously?"

Fitz nodded. "Mr. Collins did a lot of research into political contributions, making the correlation between the people at the college and various campaign funds. The old man did his homework and he kept records of everything he found. Remember that list you found with dates and initials?" I nodded. "Years ago, Mr. Collins still trusted his son, and Mrs. Burge still trusted her daughter. They directed the children to file deeds and titles for them. Some were done, some weren't, and Mr. Collins kept notes about who did what and who didn't do it. He was right not to trust them."

I thought of poor Mr. Collins, spending his time trying to make sure the land he loved would be preserved and instead finding corruption and greed everywhere he turned. No wonder he didn't trust the police. No wonder he sounded so paranoid. "I hope something good comes of this," I murmured.

"If nothing else, the entire construction project is on hold until the wills can be processed, and while the investigation continues. There will be no construction for several years, if any."

Ben raised his wine glass. "Here's to the Sierra Club. Long may they fight the good fight."

"Hear, hear." I flourished my glass, then sipped again, peering at Fitz over the rim. "So where does that leave you? It might be awkward for you."

Fitz didn't appear worried. "I acted in the best interest of the college. If they have a problem with that, perhaps I can find a job at the Community College."

"Now just a minute," I said. "I've got a lock on that job."

"What about George?" Ben asked. "I hate to ask, but he is my brother-in-law, even though he is an asshole."

"George will be reprimanded, his license revoked, and he'll be prohibited from practicing any form of legal activity." Fitz swirled the red wine in his glass. "He won't go to jail, though. I pulled a few strings to make sure of that."

Ben sighed. "That means he'll be hitting me up for money soon."

"Maybe not." Fitz took a sip of wine. "In Mr. Collins' revised will, there is a provision for George. He stands to inherit the old man's collection of books."

"Books?" I looked at Charlotte and Ben, wondering if they made any sense of such an odd bequest. They both shook their heads.

"Apparently George and the old man chatted often about literature." Fitz smiled at me. "I doubt whether George cared about literature at all, but apparently he absorbed enough details to appear informed."

"Like my Social Literature class," I murmured.

"Exactly. I suspect he got the idea from you.

George made sure he knew enough about Mr. Collins' area of interest—nineteenth-century British fiction—to appear like a talented amateur. The book collection is extensive. If he doles out the books at auction a few at a time, they should be able to live adequately on the proceeds."

"You don't know Lydia," Ben said gloomily.

"Maybe the threat of a jail sentence will keep George in line." Fitz raised the wine bottle and refilled my glass. "Do I have your forgiveness?"

"I'm still not sure I understand everything that happened." I peered at him over the rim. "It may take me a while to process it all."

"I'm available to answer questions," he said promptly.

"But can I believe what you say?"

"Of course you can." He raised his glass in a toast. "Trust me."

Nature Girl Defends the Goldfish

Many of our readers are aware of the fact that Nature Girl has, once again, expanded her family to include several Finned Friends of the Gold Fish variety. Said FF are swimming contentedly in Nature Girl's new pond in the gardens of the *Chateau de Fille Nature*.

Last week, a Pond Crisis was narrowly averted—the chemical balance of the pond had gone askew (due to dumbness on the part of NG). A quick trip to the Wet Pet Fish Store resulted in the Magic Chemical Enzyme, which righted the chemical imbalance. <whew>. Crisis averted.

NG was relaxing next to the pond after performing the weekly water tests (which confirmed that the crisis was averted) when she noticed an odd stick in the water. No, an odd stick bouncing around in the pond. No, IT WAS A SNAKE!!!!!

She leapt into attack mode; no way was a lousy snake going to eat the FF (all of whom proved that they have brains of one molecule or less because they merrily swam around, oblivious to the Evil Intruder in their midst). Grabbing the trusty dowels (used to pull Icky Things from the pond), she whapped at the snake, who slithered ACROSS THE SURFACE (certain Christians could do that, right?) of the pond and burrowed under some rocks at the side of the pond. She proceeded to whap on the rocks, trying to drive it out in order to snag it with sticks.

The FF, in the meantime, took the whapping to mean that it was food time, because taps on the rocks have meant that in the past. They queued up in their Food Spot, dangerously exposed to the Vermin in the Pond. NG hastily tossed food to them, luring them to the other side of the pond. Then, without thought of injury or Care for Self, she promptly moved the rocks to expose THE EVIL ONE. The BIG Evil One.

It slithered to the bottom of the pond. Panic. How to get it out? She began snatching plants (all of whom are floaters and thus, not attached, so to speak) and tossed them onto the beach. The FF were merrily chomping away on fish flakes, oblivious to the lurking Beast of 10,000 fathoms (okay, .5 fathom, maybe). NG saw it, coiled around the bottom, near the pump. Taking a deep breath, she plunged a hand into the pond (yes, dumb, because NG had no idea what kind of snake it was. But the FF were in danger, so into danger she went).

Perhaps the sight of a disembodied hand coming toward it awakened primal fears of octopi, because the snake slithered upward and flopped up onto the bank, facing NG. It proceeded to coil up and HISS (how dare it!), and she got her first good look at it.

At least two feet long, maybe longer; black, with long yellow stripes; about an inch wide, maybe fatter. Nasty thing. NG plunged at it with her dowels, undoubtedly appearing like an aging Zorro with wooden sticks. It slithered into the water again, and she once again started pulling plants and diverting the FF, who had polished off their krill and were bobbing around, searching for more. She flung some pellets at them; they probably talked about this all night—"wow, good chow today, I wonder why"; "Maybe that big floating stick had something to do with it, who knows?"

She probed and poked for ten minutes but couldn't find it. She even (shudder) rolled up her pants and cautiously got into the pond to feel around the pump (first putting on garden gloves lest the damn thing bite her).

No, somehow, it slithered away while her back was turned. She lifted the rocks (surprising a few toads, who jumped into the pond. She then had to capture and release them—my, they are slippery little dudes, aren't they?) When NG was finally convinced that the Evil One was gone, she collapsed on the bank, watched by the still hungry FF.

What the heck. She tossed them some more krill and poured herself a glass of wine and sat down and congratulated herself on surviving the attack of the Beast of .5 Fathoms.

The Evil One has not been sighted since. She can only hope that she convinced it that This Is Not The Pond For You and You Are Not Wanted Here. NG rearranged some of the rocks so Evil Ones cannot sunbathe there, nor can they hide out and surprise those who enjoy ponds. A quick study of her books assured her that this was a garter snake—lethal to FF, but not to NG.

Let this be a lesson to us all. Ponds, while nice, can harbor Not So Nice Visitors. Passports should be required, so we could examine them at the border and reject those we don't want.

However, this is Nature, and it just don't work that way.

J L Wilson

A word about the author…

J L Wilson is a Midwestern author who writes "mysteries with a touch of romance…and romance with a touch of gray." She can be found out and about on the Interwebs at various spots. For more details, check her Facebook page:

(https://www.facebook.com/jayeAtplay/)

or her website:

(jayellwilson.com).

And if you want to read a Nature Girl story (or two) and if you want to find out Who's Who in this story, go to her website for more details.

Thank you for purchasing
this publication of The Wild Rose Press, Inc.

For questions or more information
contact us at
info@thewildrosepress.com.

The Wild Rose Press, Inc.
www.thewildrosepress.com

To visit with authors of
The Wild Rose Press, Inc.
join our yahoo loop at
http://groups.yahoo.com/group/thewildrosepress/